Meteorites

METEORITES

STORIES

Julie Paul

BRINDLE
AND GLASS

An imprint of TouchWood Editions
TOUCHWOODEDITIONS.COM

Edited by Kate Kennedy
Cover design by Tree Abraham
Interior design by Colin Parks
Author photo by Ryan Rock

LIBRARY AND ARCHIVES CANADA CATALOGUING IN PUBLICATION

Meteorites : stories / Julie Paul.
Paul, Julie, 1969–
Canadiana (print) 20190053410 | Canadiana (ebook) 20190053429
ISBN 9781927366820 (softcover) | ISBN 9781927366837 (PDF)
Classification: LCC PS8631.A8498 M48 2019 | DDC C813/.6—DC23

We gratefully acknowledge the financial support of the Government of Canada through the Canada Book Fund and the Canada Council for the Arts, and of the Province of British Columbia through the British Columbia Arts Council and the Book Publishing Tax Credit.

PRINTED IN CANADA AT FRIESENS

23 22 21 20 19 · 1 2 3 4 5

For Ryan and Avery Jane

In memory of
Dorothy Marguerite Paul,
1926–2018

CONTENTS

As a ghost, you should be nimble. You should mosey, kick up your heels, do the boot-scootin' boogie.

Instead you can only float—you're a sickly grey balloon, attached to my rapidly burning wrist. So nice of you to join me on Hāpuna Beach, Dad.

Alo-fuckin-ha.

Is this better than yesterday's paranormal form? You wrapped around me like greasy waxed paper, rustling every time I moved in my airplane seat, as if to say, *No one goes to Hawaii alone.*

No, it is not in any way better. Today I'm expected to lie here on my towel and enjoy myself, with you as a ghost balloon, bobbing around, emitting your old-dog sigh that makes me want to scream. How am I supposed to catch the perfect wave, never mind some girly action?

I keep looking to see if anyone can see you, but no one's paying any attention. What if they did? These soft-bellied, lobster-complexioned, hibiscus-butted, once-a-year boogie boarders might just watch—and cheer—as I cut your string. Then again, they might put me under citizen's arrest. Sue this little father-son team for ruining their precious vacations.

Maybe I'll get rid of you another way: ignore the surfer-boy lifeguards, warning everyone to be cautious in the water. Spinal injuries are Hāpuna's specialty, so surely the waves can set you free. This morning, we've been informed over loudspeakers, someone was taken to hospital.

To top off the torment, amid all of this, the two beautiful women beside us are plotting their perfect imaginary futures as millionaires. It's not as if I have an actual love life, so this is what it's come to—eavesdropping on ladies in bikinis.

I know you don't want to listen, Dad, but what can you do? You're stuck.

"Yes," the one in navy says. "I would be a total raving *biatch*."

The one in turquoise shrieks, agreeing.

The lists begin. "Ten children," says Navy. "And afterwards, a boob job, because my tits would be stretched out beyond recognition."

Turquoise hoots. "Totally!"

"A cool nanny. An ice cream shop. Three personal assistants."

Okay, so maybe I've chosen the wrong women to crush on. Time to face the waves.

Except the lifeguards are flashing past me and into the water, where it looks like a dead man's washed up. In an instant, a spinal board's beneath him, straps around torso and thighs. Another guy struggles out of the sea, pink and coughing, trying to yell as he struggles toward our little patch of beach.

No. Toward the girls. He's theirs! And so is the guy strapped down. Hāpuna Beach, casualty #2.

Turquoise is up and running toward the spinal-boarded guy, slipping, screaming, "Ethan! Ethan!" over and over, then tripping after the lifeguards as they carry him away from the chomping sea.

I feel like I've been kicked in the gut.

Why the hell should I care? I have no stake in these lives. But here's the thing: I've heard their future plans—the wealth, the wanton use of money for ice cream, nannies, boob jobs. No longer will one of them live out a potential future that I can scoff at; I have to revise my vision to include a wheelchair, mushy vegetables, pool exercises, diapers.

I have to feel sorry for them.

I know that life. You made us all experts.

You're right, Dad. I *should* thank you. It's excellent résumé material. I don't know what I was thinking.

IIIIIIIIIIIIIIIIIIIIIIIIIIIII

Since Hāpuna was an epic fail, I'm driving us south.

After a late lunch in Kona, this slow, winding road toward the famous black sand beaches is doing a number on my gut. The surf's quieter, but the wind's gone fierce. Dirty sea turtles slump on the sand as if stranded. The seaside plants are the colour of lettuce, the ocean choppy, too blue.

Don't you find it funny, me using the insurance money for Hawaii—the worst place on earth, according to you? A hotbed of self-indulgence. Rich Americans in muumuus, drunk by noon.

What, no retort? We haven't seen even one muumuu.

Even dead, you have selective hearing. Or maybe you don't think Hawaii's so bad anymore. Maybe you're ready for retirement now. Maybe you secretly wanted to travel, to see the world beyond your chair.

It's common for quads to have shorter lifespans—their systems are so compromised that death can come quickly, but when you got a bad cold, we didn't worry. Then it worked into pneumonia, and inside of three weeks, you were gone. Twelve long years after the accident that claimed your spine from C1–C2 and right on down, when you drove that snowmobile into a tree.

I'll be honest with you. We never asked this out loud, but we thought it, every day: Why did you live? Did you offer anything more than a caged pit bull would? All we saw was the suffering: our suffering, caused by you.

I guess all you saw were three young boys with legs that could kick and run, arms that could carry wood and laundry, spines that bent and straightened like picture wire. Day in, day out, we thumped and wrestled above you, or peeled an orange in front of you, or finally, when we got old enough to know we could, walked away from your yelling altogether.

I thought I'd left all that behind. This trip was supposed to really make it final. And yet, here you are, stuck to me like the helium balloons we were never allowed as kids. Just my fuckin' luck.

People are still blabbing on about how we abandoned Mom, but I think she likes it up North. Yeah, maybe we did all flee when you kicked the can, but we might've stayed if you hadn't made us sell every bit of fun on wheels or runners after your accident. Very smart of you to keep us from playing hockey or baseball. Baseball! What harm could come from that? Honestly, we hated that beige house in the middle of nowhere that held us all captive, just like you.

I guess that's a bit extreme. We could sit on the toilet ourselves, pull on our own goddamned pants, take our cocks into our hands, or help other hands do that. But you made sure we felt as guilty as hell about it.

It, being life. Normality. Mobility.

Maybe if I take you to the island's highest point, the altitude will do something. Or maybe, like a bad smell, you'll just blow away.

‖‖‖‖‖‖‖‖‖‖‖‖‖‖‖‖‖‖‖‖‖‖‖‖

This whole island was begat from lava, osseous black debris everywhere, as if the dinosaurs had suffered from digestive issues, but up on Mauna Kea—tallest mountain in the world, from base to tip, according to the slick tourist mags, with the brightest stars in the USA—the ancient lava rock is a rusty brown-purple and crumbly to the touch. No one's supposed to touch it.

I have to touch it. It's all there is to walk on.

Three telescopes wait outside the gift shop, but the sky's just beginning to yield stars. Inside, a documentary drones on about the gigantic telescopes at the summit, another three thousand feet beyond the reach of my rental car. I've only begun to smell the plumeria soap when I hear a familiar voice.

"OMG, you have to get that," the voice says. "It's totally adorbs!"

It's them. Navy talking to Turquoise, who is, incredibly, smiling. I scan the crowded shop for the men, and there they are, standing near the door, looking bored. The victim—Ethan, isn't it?—sports a neck brace, but otherwise, he appears unaffected by his close call.

Wham! Anger hits me like a rogue wave. He's okay. He got away with what looks like just a little whiplash.

I'm a monster. This man's been given his life back! And yet, I'm angry?

I am, but not at him. I'm mad at you. Or maybe it's at both of you. I can't tell anymore.

But I know this: you're dead. And I'm not.

You're dead, Dad! It's time for you to go.

In a second, though, my anger vanishes, replaced by a calm wash. You're dead, and I'm alive, and my whole life is spilling out ahead of me, a path of slow-moving lava that I'll walk upon when it cools—the very ground being made before me!

Outside the gift shop, I peer into the darkening sky. So it's not as amazing as the brochures advertise; it doesn't matter. When the laser pointer caresses a constellation, I say *wow*, along with the rest of the crowd.

I stole a souvenir penknife five minutes ago. I'm gonna cut you off my wrist.

Except, as soon as I begin, before I so much as break the skin, you turn to stone—a literal stone—around my neck. A stone ghost on a heavy chain, something that can't be cut through.

Fuckity fuck. I can't keep up.

Why can't you haunt my dreams like a normal ghost?

|||||||||||||||||||||||||||||||

It's a new day. Day Four of my Hawaiian vacation, and despite a sweaty, sleepless night, there is live lava to be seen. East of the turtles, it's begun to flow right through a small town.

Let's go.

I smell smoke before I see lava, inching through a stand of trees, a few of them on fire. I park, then slip between two bunga-lows until I'm facing the scalloped edge of the slowly advancing flow, hints of bright orange beneath a layer of black. The place feels deserted, evacuated.

When I see a golf bag leaning against a tree, I don't hesitate. I grab a driver and, at the lava flow's edge, with its soundtrack of burning wood in the background, extend my arm until club meets molten. It feels like I'm touching both terminals of a car battery with wet hands; like the first time I pushed my tongue into a girl's mouth.

I am touching the centre of the earth.

With sweat coming from everywhere it can, I pull the driver out, and the lava that sticks to it burns bright orange for a minute before dimming and hardening, like an apple dipped in greying caramel. I hope it's still hot enough to burn through your chain, but before I can lift it up to my neck, a man starts yelling.

"Hey! Get outta there!"

He looks like a cowboy vigilante, standing behind a low gate like it's a saloon door, but he's waving his arms around, bearing no visible weapons.

"Put it down," he says. "Please. Come on, man, drop it."

I don't drop the heavy club, although it wants to fall, as if the jagged bit of lava on it needs to get back to where it came from. Instead I hold it out to the side, a weapon if I need it, even if it looks like the guy's more likely to cry than hurt me.

"You're breaking the law," he says. "Plus, you just don't do that to Pele. This is our sacred land. Our goddess. You want me to piss in your holy water?"

I'd seen a painting of Pele in the guidebook. A hot, red-haired beauty. At this, I let the club's head rest on the grass. "I didn't mean disrespect," I say. "I just—I was doing it for my father."

The man looks around. He can't see you.

"He's passed," I say. "Ended up a quad before he went. Couldn't lift a finger, let alone a driver."

The man nods. He even looks a little sad.

"His one wish was to see lava, in person," I lie. I raise the club like a sceptre toward the dusky sky. "So here I am," I say. "Showing him."

"Okay, man," the guy says. "Sorry about your dad. But if you don't go, the feds will bust your ass. This is private property, not to mention, you know, Pele."

Suddenly he's got a shotgun, and it's making its way up to shoulder height.

"Got it." My sweaty hands drop the club right where I'm standing, and I back away, hands up. Once there's a bit of distance between him and me, I make a run for the car.

Did you hear that, Dad? Private property. Just like me.

You're not welcome here. Please, just let me break the chain. Bury you in this creek of lava, heading to the sea. Maybe you always wanted to see the ocean but never got there. Let me go, and you'll get some prime waterfront. Please!

I'm just so exhausted. I wrap my arms around the steering wheel and rest my head on my hands. We had a funeral, but is it more praying you want? Invocations?

Okay, then. Dear Pele, Grant eternal rest unto this man tormenting me. Let him find peace in the afterlife. Amen.

When I open my eyes, you're not around my neck anymore.

Wait.

Those pathetic prayers actually worked?

You've gotta be kidding me. Now you're a tattoo on my forearm: a man astride a motorbike, and behind you, your passenger, a red-haired goddess. As you try to ride away on what looks like a classic Harley, flames on tank and fender, both of you are flipping me the bird.

It took three months for Margo to learn that Joel was an identical twin. Her mercurial, decent, generous husband—who, on the first day they met, had resisted her charms for about an hour before inviting her to stay for dinner et cetera at his lakeside cottage—was, and *is*, rather good at keeping things to himself.

Well, she can be good at that too.

Not true. Up until this month, she's been a horrible confidante: secrets feel like bees inside of her, and after all, if a person has bees in her house, isn't it best just to open the door?

Whatever. Everything has changed. Margo's been housing an enormous secret for weeks and hasn't spilled the beans. Beans? Bees are better.

This morning, Joel's brother Michael is driving toward their house. The last time the twins spoke was ten years ago, in 1988, after a tragedy involving a girl they both loved, a fire followed by a suicide, and implications that Michael was responsible. Joel doesn't talk about it, but Margo knows he misses his brother. Doesn't he? He must—he's his brother! She doesn't have siblings so the whole thing is entirely foreign to her, but surely they aren't meant to stay estranged. There are laws of nature about this kind of thing. And how could someone truly be responsible for someone else's suicide?

It isn't only Margo who believes this whole thing has gone on long enough: their dying father Bill out in Parksville is bucket-listing, and at the top of the list, above seeing the endangered orcas in Victoria, is having his sons reunite. "Please try," Bill said to her on the phone last month, a rarity for him to even talk, let alone to her. "Knowing they've made up would give me a bit of peace before I go."

She couldn't refuse a dying man's wishes, so that very day, she'd emailed Michael via the Vancouver gallery that represents him, and he'd responded within the hour, and voila, the thing was set in motion. He would "drop in" to their house after visiting the town north of Toronto where they grew up—a three-hour drive from them. She likes the way he writes. "It would be an honour to meet you and little Evelyn," he said. They've both agreed to keep it to themselves, not even letting Bill or the twins' mother, Jean, know, in case things turn ugly. She's seen Joel's temper flare; they might have that in common.

Margo hasn't kept the secret entirely to herself. She's been whispering the facts of it to Evie—eighteen months old and already such a good listener, even if she isn't quite up to snuff on responding in actual words. The other day she sang her secret to Evie to the tune of "Mary Had a Little Lamb," which made Evie scrunch up her brow in confusion, the way Joel does.

Does Michael do the same? Are their voices the same? Does he share Joel's love for classic rock? Do they, she wonders, as all the girls must have, measure up *all the way down*? She feels herself blushing, but how can she not go there? Her husband has a body double. Oh, Jesus.

|||||||||||||||||||||||||||||||

Douchebag. Doofus. Asshat. Horndog. Dickwad.

Doofus was Joel's go-to label for Mike back in the day, whenever he jerked his chain, but since Mike left, he's been cycling through all of these endearments in his head. It makes him feel better.

Their mother, out with Pops in their West Coast retirement village, calls it childish, Mike and him not talking for all these years. She got it, at first, but it seems her patience has run out. Yeah, Joel's still pissed off, but he's been working on it, quietly, making internal strides year by year, name-calling aside, into letting go of the whole stupid thing.

He's seen the photos: Mike's obviously still dealing with it too, processing *his* stuff there on his canvases for everyone to see—and buy, if they've got a spare twenty thousand. The last time Jean mailed Joel a picture of Mike, some schmoozy shot taken at an awards thing, he looked light-deprived, worn out. Is that what the coast does to people? Rich fucks like him were supposed to look tanned and buff, just back from a vacation.

Joel's never had a vacation, ever, but up until they moved a year ago, he'd had the lake at his door. Now there's a lake just down the road, and Evie's a bundle of giggles and energy, and his "exotic" wife, Margo—other peoples' word, not his—loves their new house in this new-to-them town that shouldn't have ghosts. He no longer sees Christina's blonde head in the bank lineups like he did back home; he doesn't hear scattershot laughter and get a gut ache when it isn't her.

So what's that feeling he has, when he's alone in his wood shop? A pulling sensation. A chill when he normally runs hot. Someone watching him.

Is it her, wanting them to make up, like in that cheesy movie, *Ghost*?

Likely, he's just going a little crazy.

Joel knows that Mike believes he was always Christina's top choice, but it isn't true. There was that day when the three of them were studying for math at their place, right after she and Mike started dating. Studying started by watching *Three's Company* and other garbage on the two channels they got. Then Mike got called into work at the Chinese restaurant last minute, so that left Joel and Christina. He remembered their old agreement: if they were able to fool them, they could kiss each other's girlfriends. There was no fooling Christina, obviously—the three of them had been friends for years—but Joel ignored that part of it.

Video Hits came on, Madonna baring it all, and there they sat like old folks, covered up with Jean's latest afghan.

"You want some Quik?" he asked her, during a boring Depeche Mode video.

She smiled at him. "Want what quick?" Always the wordsmith.

He blushed. "Um. You know, chocolate milk."

"Sure," she said. "Want some help?"

"No, I got it." He also had an instant erection.

As Joel stirred the powder into the big glasses of milk, he made a deal with himself: if she took the glass with Bugs Bunny on it, he'd kiss her; if she took the plain one, he wouldn't.

Back in the living room, she was on the phone. "Be home around eight," she was saying. "I'll do the stalls then, Dad. Bye!"

"Machine?" he asked.

She nodded. "Luckily, or else I'd have to go home and help. Your parents are at work, right? And it's okay if I stay like we planned? Mike said he could give me a ride home later."

"Dad doesn't get home till sixish. Mom's at a Tupperware conference in Toronto. And I can drive you."

"Hello, Bugsy." She reached with her elegant hand to take the glass. "Thank you."

"No problem." He was red again.

Joel sat down in the same place as before, but there seemed to be less space; he had to put his arm behind her so he wouldn't bump her glass of chocolate milk. He had to kiss her. A deal is a deal.

They necked until they heard Bill's car pull into the driveway, then scrambled to separate ends of the couch and pretended to be interested in the news.

Joel doesn't know whether he could have kept Christina from dying. But he returns to this moment on bad days, when he wishes he'd made more of a move, somehow, and kept her from getting more serious with Mike, who'd been poaching his girlfriends since middle school.

Horndog. Douchebag.

He's still not ready to make up with the jerk.

|||||||||||||||||||||||||||||||||

"What's shaking, Joely-boy?" The woman behind the counter has flour on her forehead and an apron covered in smears of what Michael hopes is only chocolate. She gives him a once-over. "Who died?"

"Hello," he says. "And, actually, I'm Joel's brother. Michael."

The woman's jaw drops; he hasn't seen that response in a decade.

"No shit," she says. "I mean, hello. Welcome. I'm Vi. Where are you coming from, son?"

"Vancouver," he says.

She whistles. "That explains your get-up. I've never seen your brother out of jeans."

"You know him well, then," Michael says. "I'm, well, I'm surprising him for a visit, and I want to bring some food, and so . . . "

"They get my cinnamon buns, mostly. Sometimes a chicken pot pie. Margo's got her hands full with that little one."

"Lovely. I'll take both." Jean would be proud of him: never showing up empty-handed is one of her rules. Another is to never show up unannounced. He's one for two.

"Say hello to your brother," Vi says. "And that little chocolate family of his."

Something he hasn't heard much in a decade, either: *Brother.*

He can't quite believe how Joel's settled down already, and with a wife such as this. His mother showed him their wedding photos a couple of years ago, just after she'd received them: they'd eloped in Algonquin Park although, to Michael, she looks like she'd be much more at home in a sparkling ballroom.

"Quite the curls, eh?" his mother had said. "Her father's Jamaican."

"She's stunning," he said. "Where'd he find her?"

"She found *him*. Came to the lake to buy some chairs, out from Toronto."

"He's still making those damned things?" Joel had started making wooden furniture when they were teens, Muskoka chairs for the cottagers around the lake and bookshelves for the locals, and from what Jean had told him, he'd moved on to more general carpentry.

"Not sure," she said. "But they got him a wife, so that's something."

His paintings, so far, have yielded many women of varying ethnicities (none made of chocolate, Vi), although he's learned not to lead with that question. But a wife? Or love? No sign of anything like that at all.

Mike and Joel Schaefer, matching sons of Bill and Jean, insurance salesman and Tupperware lady, respectively, were once citizens in a cosmos of two, one in red, the other in blue. Five floorboards separated their beds until they could jump across the gap, bed to bed, cheering each time they made it.

Joel and Mike, Mike and Joel. From one egg to one room in the uterus, to eighteen years in that bedroom in a small house at the bottom end of Ontario, in Jackson's Point, beside Lake Simcoe, a gigantic, almost-Great Lake, Ice Fishing Capital of Canada, to this—a ten-year gap—how was that possible?

Back then, life was simple and good, scrapes and bruises, blanket forts and fishing for poop in the toilet; card houses and wolf calls and waterskiing and complaining about chores. The good working-class life, with dinner in front of the TV on Friday night. Mike and Joel, Joel and Mike—special because they were the same. Everyone they met told them so, after saying they were lucky to have a "built-in best friend." Sappy, but also true.

When girls entered the picture, they found them cute, adorable, matchy-matchy, although Joel had a slightly wider mouth, and Mike's brow furrowed more. Joel, shyer, walked with his head just a bit more stooped. Mike—it was just a fact, not a brag—had a little more luck with the girls. They sometimes switched T-shirts at the school dance to see if anyone would notice. They fooled people when Mike reminded Joel to stand up straighter.

They got to know Christina in Grade 10, and over the next two years, in her Smiths T-shirts and long skirts, coming into town on the school bus from her farm, writing poetry in the back seat, reciting it from the top of picnic tables, she was their friend, nothing more.

Christina, who seemed to burn through each day like she was being chased, a flurry of gestures and scarves and limbs, eyes shooting blue flames at whatever she focused on, and for a brief moment in time, it was *him*—still Mike then, not yet Michael Schaefer, artist.

But Christina is dead now and has been for ten years. So why does she haunt him? He's done the research into sensing spirits, something more acceptable to mention on the West Coast, and from what he can tell, those shadows he sees from his peripheral vision are possibly her. Ditto the sudden sinking feeling in his belly when everything otherwise is fine, or the sense that he's got insects buzzing beneath his skin.

Apparently, she's trying to convey a message. He'd like her to stop it: he knows he messed up. But she's the one who killed herself, months after the fire, even after he told her he'd keep on loving her, no matter what her face looked like. She'd seen his shocked expression, though, when she pulled back the scarf she'd been hiding beneath, the one and only time he saw her after the fire.

He'd like her to go, now, to rest in peace, so he can do the same. But if wishes were horses, as Jean used to say when he and Joel had circled half the Sears Wish Book for their Christmas lists, beggars would ride.

||||||||||||||||||||||||||||||

Saturday mornings, Margo usually gets to stay in bed while Joel does Evie-care and breakfast, and she only comes out when she smells cinnamon or sausage. But today she's getting up with Joel, even though Evie was awake half the night teething.

"You're not exhausted?" he asks.

"My back is sore," she says. It's a lie. "It feels better when I'm moving."

"It wasn't from me, I hope," he says, pulling her to his chest. "Or maybe more of that would help?"

She kisses him lightly on the lips. "Maybe later," she says. "I'm thinking more about a hot shower."

The heat does nothing good for her hair or skin or the bags under her eyes—*my bags have purses*, her mother likes to say—but it's the only place she can gather her thoughts, alone, and give her a few minutes in which she won't be tempted to tell Joel that Michael is on his way.

Gah! She's so nervous. What will he think of her? She shouldn't care, but she's never met a brother-in-law before. She wants to impress him, and not embarrass Joel; she wants to know

everything about him and what happened to drive them apart—
all Joel has said is that Michael messed up, not only stealing a
girl from him but worse, and it ended in suicide. What does that
even mean, and will Michael tell her? She's not sure she's going to
be able to keep her cool. Never mind *her* cool, what about Joel's?
He might just lose it when his brother walks through the door.

IIIIIIIIIIIIIIIIIIIIIIIIIIIIIIII

On that Saturday afternoon, when Mike was at Christina's barn,
Joel was supposed to be studying. He took a joint out of Mike's
drawer, smelled it, felt its paper skin and the strands of plants
inside. It was just plants. An herbal remedy. That was most likely
why Christina wanted to try it; he knew she'd never touch a
cigarette, not with all the crap they put in them. But herbs—she
was into that sort of thing. She wore a crocheted bag around her
neck, all the colours of the rainbow, filled with stones that were
supposed to make her more creative. Once, she placed a stone in
his hand.

"Lapis lazuli," she said.

"Is that some kind of spell?"

"No, silly. That's the name of the stone."

The rock, bright blue, felt warm in his hands. Her warmth. It
was the colour of her eyes condensed into solid form.

He could have smoked it then, that slender joint: he had it
between his lips. He could have put himself out of his misery and
gotten a serious buzz going, so that when Michael came home
after work, after being at Christina's, after having sex with her,
after getting high, *he* would have been the one feeling good.

But what Joel did was return to his Chemistry 12 textbook,
until the most terrible phone call of his life blasted through
his concentration.

||||||||||||||||||||||||||||||||

Of course, Michael misses Joel—they shared a womb. They were best buds from the get-go.

But after Christina died, everything changed. It was like he was seeing things on a screen, in pixels, as if all of life were filtered, divided into little segments, none of them including his twin.

He took off for the West Coast, the farthest reach. The world he moved to was stacked boxes, apartments, little cubes of life, and when he wasn't waiting tables to pay for it, he painted tiny boxes on huge canvases, dividing the space into smaller and smaller squares because it made him feel better. It was what he knew. They were manageable little objects, like rocks in a river: if he reached one, he was safe. He had to leave it, eventually, but he could move on to another.

Day by day, canvas by canvas, he was able to keep going like that.

Maybe he'd tapped into some kind of communal need because people started noticing his work; or maybe they just liked the pretty colours. Then, thanks to his mentor, Ron, he got a show in a big gallery, but he still felt like he was just surviving, doing what he had to do to keep himself moving forward.

Before he started winning prizes and fellowships and bought this condo, far above the streets, he buried Mike and became Michael Schaefer and, like so many people in Vancouver, dug his roots into the sky.

At the beginning of Grade 12, he and Christina started dating. In early October, she took him to Toronto to visit her aunt and they ended up at the AGO. He'd never been to an art gallery—he didn't know that galleries were for anything other than selling stuff. But there they were, wandering past incredible work, just to look and feel.

She introduced Michael to the Group of Seven first. He thought Lawren Harris's white mountains, peeking from behind dark hills, looked like the abominable snowman from *Rudolph the Red-Nosed Reindeer*. When he told Christina this, she kissed him and called him a weirdo. Then they went their separate ways so she could write an assignment without distraction, and he ended up in the Henry Moore room.

He walked around each of those giant women, reclining, sitting awkwardly, and seemed to recognize them. Maybe that was normal, recognizing someone in Moore's work—the universal in the specific, all of that—but to Michael, they embodied his mother, Jean. Taller than most women, but bigger-boned and angular too, and like Moore's reclining figures, leaning on one hand, she couldn't fully relax.

He loved them. Started imagining what it would be like to be famous like this, known for capturing someone's essence in stone, or on canvas. It was the first hint of the strangest notion he'd ever had: he wanted to become an artist.

On Thanksgiving Sunday, they smoked up in the hayloft at Christina's farm. It was only the second time they'd done it, and after a few tokes each, they started making out. What was left of the joint, Michael set on a beam beside him. They were giddy, relaxed, totally turned on. Afterward, they both fell asleep, just for a little nap, and when his watch beeped its alarm, Christina didn't stir.

Before leaving, he had a couple more tokes to finish up, but when it started to burn his fingers, he dropped the tiny roach. He searched for it—nowhere to be found. After waiting another couple minutes to make sure everything was okay, he left Christina sleeping, more relaxed than he'd ever seen her, her face peaceful, aglow. He had to get to work on time, so he gave no more thought to the fallen butt. There was no smoke, no fire, nothing to worry about except being late for work.

||||||||||||||||||||||||||||||

From the bedroom, Joel hears a vehicle pull into the driveway, then, as he always does, checks from the window to see who's at the wheel. What the fuck?

Mike. His brother is getting out of a silver SUV with two white bakery boxes and a liquor store bag. In a grey blazer. On a Saturday. In June.

Before he can stop her, Margo answers the door in her post-shower attire—just a t-shirt turban wrapping her wet hair above her silky peach kimono. She shrieks a welcome that will surely wake Evie from her late-morning nap.

"Oh, my God! Michael! Come in! Come in!"

Michael? His name is Mike.

"Joel!" she yells up the stairs. "We've got a visitor!"

What the hell is going on? She doesn't sound surprised.

"Joel, where are you?"

He's here, but all he wants to do is hide, or climb onto the roof and descend the trellis, make his way to his shop, or better yet, drive away.

"Joel!"

He can't escape it. Joel descends the old creaking stairs, and sees Mike, standing in his hallway, as pale as in the photograph. Is he going to faint?

"Hey," Joel says.

Margo's lit up like she's won the lottery. She knew. How could she not prepare him for this?

"Long time, no see." Mike sticks out his hand for a shake he doesn't want to return. His hand is cold, smooth—are his nails actually polished?

"You went to Vi's, I see."

"Just a little something. She thought I was you, going to a funeral."

"Ha!" Perfect. Now everyone in town would know about this.

Evie starts wailing from upstairs, a sudden siren. Mike looks startled.

"I'll go," Joel and Margo say at the same time.

"No, I'll go," she says. "I've got to get dressed anyway."

She's right about that.

"I'll give you the tour," Joel says, defaulting to what he always does when visitors arrive. And why shouldn't he show off his hundred-and-twenty-year-old house and all the renovations he's done in a year? It's not in any glossy magazine, and won't win a huge award, but he's proud of it. And *Michael* better be an appreciative audience.

He is. He notices the craft, the details, the work Joel's completed. Doesn't overreact at the nasty counters and cupboards in the untouched kitchen—the next room on the reno list, once they can afford something better than laminate.

"Check it out," Joel says, pointing at the lozenge-shaped gilded frame on the hallway ceiling. "Apparently there was an artist going door-to-door, back in the day. There are a few specimens still intact."

The painting is a strange representation of a beaver that looks more like a cross between a jackrabbit and a cougar, around which the artist painted faux-marble tiles in grey and black. It's sort of ugly, but it was part of what charmed him into buying this old house.

Mike nods. "Impressive."

He's still being polite. When will that groomed composure start to crack?

Half an hour later, Mike's standing on Joel's back deck, laughing with his finally clothed wife, playing peek-a-boo with his daughter, and it's Joel's composure under threat. His muscles feel like they're turning to bone, his hands forming tight fists he's not sure he'll be able to control if Mike touches Margo's arm once more. And yet he's making goddamned iced tea for them all to drink in the sun and pretend that everything is normal.

"I have an idea," Mike says, while Margo is in the house changing Evie after their tea party lunch of the food he brought from Vi's. "I'd like your help with it."

Joel nods as minutely as possible, stares out into the trees, stone-faced.

"I want to build something back home, for Christina."

Joel's head whips around to stare at his pale gob. "You what?"

"I'm going start a scholarship in her name, for a promising poet or artist in Grade 12. But I also want to make a kind of monument to her."

"What, like a totem pole?"

"No, bro. But something made of wood. More your area of expertise than mine."

Bro. "Park bench, then? Or maybe a miniature barn?"

Mike stops smiling at this dig. "A big book, made of wood, I was thinking," he says. "One of her poems engraved on a metal page." He rubs his forehead and pushes his hair out of his eyes. Joel's gesture. "She needs a memorial, in Jackson's Point. It's just not right to pretend that she never existed. I just came from there, Joel. It's like none of us were ever there."

This makes Joel soften a little. He imagines little kids running their hands over the words, pictures taking his own kid there, to show her and Margo the sights, go for a dip in the lake they all loved.

There was a day at the lake, at the old mansion beach, before it all went to hell. The OMB, they called it in code, the beach in front of an abandoned house where they used to hang out after school and on long summer afternoons, searing their skin in the sun and jumping from the borrowed, boggy dock into that silty green water. A day when Christina declared, "I want to live this day on a loop. This is the one day I want to repeat forever." Joel remembers thinking that this would be a fine idea. Just him, his brother, and this beautiful, smart girl. Three friends at the beach, hiding out, not getting caught, suspended in time.

"Think fast," he and Mike had said at the same time, each of them throwing her a can of Molson Canadian from the cooler, and somehow, she'd caught them both.

The twins lay on their stomachs reading comic books and drawing while she scribbled poems down in her journal. Joel had brought a ghetto blaster and played Pink Floyd and David Bowie, and they all wished they had more beer. Nothing else happened; this was pre-love, pre-choosing between them, pre-anything.

That's the point he wants to return to, the factory reset point of their lives.

Before he can stop himself, Joel blurts it out. "Do you ever, you know, feel like she's nearby?"

He's never spoken about this to anyone, ever.

Mike nods. "All the time. I see movement in the corners, or feel a change in the air, sometimes music—that song by the Smiths she loved—"

"'There is a Light that Never Goes Out.'"

"Yep." Mike moves a little closer, places his hand on Joel's shoulder. "I've missed you," he says. "No one knew her like we did."

He's getting chills again, and it isn't the weather. But this is all too fast. One afternoon and Mike thinks they're besties again. And has he completely forgotten the burden he saddled Joel with, making him promise to never tell about the final toke?

"What poem?" Joel asks.

"I've got a dozen or so," he says. "We can go through them together and choose."

"I've got one too," Joel says, and the shock on Mike's face is priceless. "Like you said, no one knew her like we did."

||||||||||||||||||||||||||||||

When Margo brings Evie out onto the deck after half an hour— she'd forced herself to stay upstairs—neither she nor Evie can stop staring at Michael. The brothers are talking, even laughing a little, and Margo can't tell their voices apart.

"Come here, little chick," Joel says, and Evie's fuzzy head nestles into his shoulder. Is that envy on Michael's face? It makes Margo tear up.

"This is your Uncle Mike," Joel says into her ear, and she turns her face out again, to see Michael. They're all looking at Michael.

It's incredible enough, seeing two people with the same face, mannerisms, and voice, but for one of them to be your husband, a singular being who is now—has always been—one of two? But it's something more. Even though he's basically a complete stranger, she feels a kinship with Michael, a sudden sense of connection beyond what she'd sensed in their few simple emails.

And okay, yes, it's impossible not to see their differences. They both work with their hands, but carpentry versus visual arts—there's a lot of space between those two. Michael is more stylish, Leonard Cohen to Joel's Bruce Springsteen. Taller, somehow, or maybe that's just the Fluevogs. Paler, trimmer, neater. Urban. He holds her gaze longer, pauses just a beat longer before responding to a question, as if "What part of Vancouver do you live in?" is the most interesting, complicated query of all time. He's touched her shoulder and arm three times during their conversations.

"I hope you'll stay here tonight," Margo says now. "We have lots of space." Joel has been hot and cold all day, a fog of coolness over him most of the time, shooting her looks of disbelief, but she caught him with tears in his eyes while he watched Michael chase Evie around the yard.

"You're so kind," he says. "But I've got a room at the Colonial Inn, out on the highway."

Joel looks at Margo, and they both shake their heads. "It's a hole," he says. "Stay here."

Is he really saying that?

Michael flips his hair out of his eyes with one quick hand, just like Joel does. "I'd be honoured," he says. Again with that word.

"Can I please make you dinner?"

"We've got it," Joel says, quickly. "Meat okay?"

Michael nods. "I'm an omnivore. Happy with anything."

"Joel's the chef around here," Margo says. "Sounds like you're a cook too?"

"I dabble," he says. "Mainly Thai and Japanese these days."

"Damn," she says. "We're more straight-up around here. Things the baby can eat, you know?"

Michael laughs and opens his hands to the sky. "I love me some Gerber's pears."

"Joel's favourite."

"Of course it is."

||||||||||||||||||||||||||||||

Joel can hear Mike and Margo talking quietly in the kitchen, finishing up the supper dishes. He and Margo are trying to keep to a routine for Evie, post-weaning, so he did the bath and bed ritual, and Evie went down much quicker than normal despite all the excitement of the day.

His brother is in the house, and his guts are a complete mess— emotional rollercoaster doesn't come close to describing it. Part of him wants to sneak away into his shop and bang the shit out of some wood, part of him still wants to punch Mike out, but he's got to face this music like an adult now.

He remembers, after it happened, how hard it actually was to stop talking to Mike back then, even holding the secret of the final toke. Because even through the blame and the fury, he was able to put himself in Mike's shoes—to know he'd hurt someone, unwittingly, and then, for worse things to happen as a fallout. And, he reminds himself, Christina had pressured Mike into getting the weed. To improve her poetry, maybe, or to defy her strict father. Even if he'd accidentally caused the fire, Mike wasn't the only one smoking up in the hayloft.

When he gets downstairs, Margo and Mike have moved to the deck in the twilight, and Joel holds onto these thoughts, these threads of compassion, while he settles into a chair on the deck with a beer. A couple of fireflies in the cedar boughs wink their way behind Mike's head—the first ones they've seen this season.

"Mosquitoes will be out soon," Margo warns. "But isn't this hour just golden?"

"You are extremely blessed," Mike says. "All of this, and Evie too."

His brother says *blessed* now? At least he hasn't asked about Margo's background, or not while he's been around. She is never thrilled when the inevitable question comes up: *But where are you really from?* This woman is from downtown Toronto. She misses shopping on Queen Street, the pakoras and shawarmas and blintzes of home. Yes, okay, she has a Jamaican father she never met.

"So you're half Jamaican," Mike says, apropos of nothing. Mom must've told him. Or else he's doing that mind-reading thing they used to do.

Margo laughs. "Fifty-fifty," she says.

"Evie seems to have gotten a fair percentage," he says. "Those giant brown eyes."

"I see Schaefer cheekbones and smile," Margo says. "But definitely my nose and naughty streak."

They all smile, Joel included, and Mike says, "We had our fair share of shit-disturbing, didn't we, Joel?"

He likely means things like colouring on the walls with magic marker or hiding for an hour in Sears while their frantic mother cried, thinking they'd been taken. But Christina just pops in ahead of these things and takes over his thinking. "You could say that," he says. "Compared to us, Evie's good as gold."

|||||||||||||||||||||||||||||||

When Michael came home that day after visiting Christina for the first time after the fire, he was in shock. He and Joel were still speaking at that point, but Joel didn't ask about it—no doubt he could tell it had been bad. After a couple of hours in his bedroom with headphones plugged into his Discman, Michael emerged and gave a quick report. Half of her face destroyed, patched badly together again, her mouth not working on that side, same with her arm. A patch over one eye. A scarf pinned to her hair, to curtain over the damage. A version of herself he barely recognized.

What he didn't say was how awful it was, what had replaced her cheek, her brow, her eyelid. He'd heard of skin grafts and remembered the smoothness of her bum—couldn't they use skin from there to fix things up?

Every time the phone rang over the holidays, Michael jumped. Joel told him he was going to go with him the next visit, even if she said no. He had to see for himself, he said. To let her know she'd get better, that they were still her buddies. She didn't call. Whenever they phoned her house, no one answered.

At the end of the first school day after Christmas, Jean met them at the door.

"They say it was depression," she told them, then started wailing.

"Mom, what is?"

Through her hysterics, they heard the news. "She shot herself, out in the barn, last night."

Michael sat down on the steps, unable to stand.

"She's gone. Christina. She's dead."

According to Christina's mother, it was the disfigurement that was too much to bear. The trouble with eating, spilling drinks out of straws, all of that was hard, she told them after the funeral. But the fact that Christina would look like that forever and see pity before anything else in people's faces—that was beyond her.

Had she left a note saying this? How did anyone know for sure?

"If only she had never been in that barn," Christina's mother said, her face grey and flat. "God knows why she ever fell asleep in there in the first place. But that girl was an explorer. She was probably writing a poem about hay and needed to go smell it."

Michael turned away so she wouldn't see his imploding face.

"You killed her," Joel said, when they were alone, his face a mess of tears. "Not a shotgun. You."

Michael doesn't know if Joel has told anyone about the spark; he hasn't said a thing. But he knows that it was the last day Joel had spoken to him, until today.

Now Michael surveys the sky, the yard, the old house, the deck—the whole dreamlike moment. Actual fireflies.

"I wish Mom and Dad could see this," he says. "Have they met you, Margo?"

"Only over the phone," she says. "But I'm thinking we should make the trip west, sooner than later. They were intending on coming to the wedding, but we eloped, so that didn't happen."

Michael nods. "It's pancreatic. They're not giving him much time."

Joel squirms in his seat. "But what about remission? That happens, right?"

Hasn't Joel talked to them lately? Or heard how quickly this one moves?

"He's stopped all treatments. It's more about . . . day-to-day, now, doing whatever he wants in the time left."

"Is that why you're here, then?" Joel says. "Bill's wish list?"

"You heard about it," Michael says. "But not entirely. I mean, I've wanted to see you for years, Joel."

"Okay. But how did you know I'd open the door at all?"

Michael shrugs. "I didn't."

The brothers lock glances for a second, then both look at Margo.

"Bill is going to be pretty stoked, you know," Margo says. "Should we call them? It's only dinner time in BC."

Joel shakes his head. "In the morning. When Evie's up to chat."

"Good plan," Margo says, then slaps her smooth calf. "Bastard mosquito got me!"

"They always do," Joel says. He gets up and reaches a hand toward her, as if Mike isn't even there. "Time to go in."

"I'll be right in," Michael says, and stays in his chair. He wants to take some photos for some future work, mostly of the magenta sky. Joel smirks at him, like he thinks he's going to light up a joint. If he had one, he might.

Once they're inside, he can hear the river, flowing half a block away, and little else. Not even a Smiths song. Maybe Christina will leave him alone now. Maybe the goosebumps on his forearms are just from the dropping temperature.

IIIIIIIIIIIIIIIIIIIIIIIIIIIIIII

Joel's bringing a second bottle of red into the living room when he feels a change in the air. There's a thickening, a pressure to it, and before Joel knows what he's doing, he sits down beside Margo on the sofa and extends his hand to pat Mike's leg—a signature Mike move—and says, "I appreciate you coming all this way. I don't really want to talk about anything, you know, from before, but I'm willing to start again, from here. For Dad."

He can see Margo wiping her eyes, and now she's taking his hand, and Mike's, and squeezing her joy into their fingers.

"You guys!" she says. "This is amazing." And then she just sits there holding both hands. Joel pulls his away, and Mike doesn't. Joel stares at his wife until she lets go. Enough already.

"Did Joel point out the painting on the ceiling?" she asks. "Our ancient beaver?"

"I told him," Joel says.

"Impressive," Mike says, again. "What year did you say the house was?"

"1894," Margo says. "I remember each time the wind howls through the attic."

"More wine?" Joel asks.

"The Prosecco I brought should be chilled by now," Mike says. "Might be time for a little celebratory bubbly?"

He doesn't feel like celebrating, let alone with some pretentious froth, but he lets Mike go pop his cork. He's doing it for Bill. But as much as their father says he wants this little reunion, it likely won't make much of a difference at all.

IIIIIIIIIIIIIIIIIIIIIIIIIIIIII

The bubbles go right to Margo's belly, never mind her head, so it feels like she's pregnant all over again. Or maybe it's a bad feeling coming over her, drinking with these guys—how long can this new peace last? And Prosecco, after four glasses of wine! Way more than her usual half-glass, what with the pregnancy, then breastfeeding.

She heads to the kitchen, red wine glasses in hand, to make up a snack plate: this much alcohol needs something to soak it up.

The radio is on, a late-night program she likes; now it's Destiny's Child's "Say My Name" making her hips move. When was the last time they went dancing? In front of the TV with Barney the purple dinosaur doesn't count.

She's prepping their go-to snack without thinking—Wheat Thins, marble cheddar, and sliced dills—but it suddenly seems inadequate. She can't even blame Evie—Joel loves this simplicity.

Michael likely eats caviar on the regular, lifted to his mouth on endive leaves by his elegant, pampered hands.

What she's seeing is an experiment's results right here and now: what happens to identical twins when the variables change. Environment versus temperament, nature versus nurture. Michael's surface is all pretty and gentle, but there's a steely layer beneath that she can sense when he's up against Joel's pragmatism, his confidence, here in his house with wife and child.

They've missed out on so much, in the missing years. To look at them, sunlight and physical work have skipped over Michael, but deeper—do they feel a gap, an empty shelf, a hollow?

She's only known Joel without his brother. Would he be different if this rift had never happened?

So many questions. But more than anything, Margo's dying to know what really happened to this Christina girl to cause this kind of damage. She wants a quiet moment with Michael alone, to ask him.

IIIIIIIIIIIIIIIIIIIIIIIIIIIIII

It feels like a mirror Joel's staring into, seeing Mike talking to Margo like that, laughing, clinking their glasses together, eating their favourite snack. Or maybe it's more like looking at his shadow.

It still feels unbelievable, having his brother here, but this is different. An out-of-body sense coming over him that it isn't his brother's hand suddenly on his wife's shoulder, but his own, just a friendly squeeze to the arm before a kiss.

And then rage hits, storming his body like a terrorist.

Talk the terrorist into backing down, Joel. Tell it to be reasonable. It's only his hand on her shoulder. A doctor might do that, or even a stranger, like the firefighter who clapped him on the back after he shoved a twenty into the big black boot for the fundraiser outside the grocery store.

Mike hasn't kissed her. He's just staring into her eyes, seeming to hang on her every word like he's done all day, and she seems to like the attention.

Joel reaches over to rub Margo's shoulders. *This is love, buddy,* he thinks. *Watch and learn.*

"When you come west, you'll have to stay with me too," Mike says. "I've just bought the condo across the hall from my original one to use as a studio, so you can choose what view you want."

"Wow," Margo says. "Joel, we really should make a plan."

"It's gonna have to be the winter," he says. "This is my busy season."

Mike is shaking his head. "I don't know if we have that much time, bro. Maybe you can't tell over the phone, but Bill really is sliding fast."

He can't handle this conversation tonight.

"I'm beat," Joel says, and stands up. "The spare bedroom's made up, and there are towels on the dresser."

"Thank you, Joel," Mike says. "Truly."

"You coming?" he asks Margo.

"In a bit," she says. "I'm too full to lie down just yet." She giggles. "And maybe a little tipsy too."

He's desperate to be alone with her, to process this insanity of a day. He's not mad at her, for any of it; he just needs to talk. And someone has to be the good hostess to this guy, who's still got energy from three time zones back.

Mike looks tanked, a look he also recognizes from the mirror. "Same here, babe."

No. He doesn't get to say that.

"Goodnight, then," Joel says. He gives Margo a wide-eyed look, but she simply waves and throws him a kiss.

|||||||||||||||||||||||||||

Michael should have stopped at the red wine. He knows better, but still, he always gets caught up in the moment, and if there ever was a moment to get caught up in, well—

Margo's taken some of the dishes, so he gathers the rest of the plates and glasses and follows her into the kitchen. He feels crunching underfoot. What the hell? Ah, right. Cheerios. There's a toddler in the house.

What a thing to be jealous of! But that's what he's feeling—for everything Joel has. He'd paint over that ceiling beaver, ASAP, get some new draperies, and make the kitchen a priority, but otherwise, this whole package has him filled to the brim with longing.

Michael pushes open the swinging kitchen door to find Margo dancing to Fatboy Slim as she gathers her curls into a ponytail in front of the sink she's filling with hot water.

"I love this song," he says, and starts singing along. "*I have to praise you like I should.*"

"My God," Margo says. "It's just too crazy, your voice and Joel's."

"This must be weird for you. It always was, back in the day."

Margo turns off the tap and faces him. "Like with Christina?"

He nods. How much does she know?

"Michael, what really happened?" she asks. "Joel hasn't told me much at all, and it seems—well, I just want to know."

"Fair enough," Michael says. He takes the dishcloth from over the tap, dips it into the soapy water so he can wipe the dreadful countertops. "I was dating her, but we were both friends with her for years. Then, one day after we were hanging out in a hayloft at her farm, she got caught in a barn fire."

"Those stains don't come off," she says. "Don't worry about it. So, you got out of the fire? And she didn't?"

He puts the cloth back over the tap. "No, I was at work by the time it happened. I'd left her there, sleeping peacefully."

"How horrible!" Margo cries. The synth music coming from the ghetto blaster does not match up with this conversation, but he's happy it's on.

"It was. One whole side of her face was burned and down her arm." He takes a deep breath. "But she was healing, slowly, and then, a few months later, she shot herself."

Margo stands there, shaking her head. "What a terrible loss."

Michael Jackson's "Remember the Time" is coming from the radio now. "The worst."

"And Joel?" she says. "He was, what, in love with her too?"

"Yeah. He wouldn't forgive me for dating her—or for not being able to save her, I guess." *Shut up now*, he tells himself. *That's all you need to say.*

"What a mess," Margo says. "But, I mean, all of this was so long ago. Will you . . . I mean, I hope you guys can move on. That he'll finally be able to let it go."

"We're making progress," Michael says. "He's talking to me again, at least."

"Yes. And Bill's going to be happy," she says. "That's the main thing right now."

She turns to face the sink again and begins to wash the dishes, her lovely neck exposed beneath her ponytail, hips swaying to the beat.

|||||||||||||||||||||||||||||||||

Joel can't sleep. He needed a break, but now he's wide awake, thinking about his father. He can actually hear music coming from downstairs. Fuck. His head is spinning, his stomach uneasy, but maybe some water will help.

Where's the water glass? It's always in the ensuite, except it isn't now.

Fine. He'll go down there, give Margo the stink eye, hydrate, and return upstairs, where he'll take a pre-emptive Tylenol and fall into a numbing slumber. Mike will have to entertain himself tonight. Surely he's got a book, or some hand lotion to lube the palm.

They were best friends once, he and Mike, no disputing it. But it hasn't felt like there's a hole in his life, with him gone. Or if it once did, it's been mended, with a mishmash of threads, and he's carried on. Today has been more of a tear; something sharp poking into him, a rent in the fabric, but he'll get over it. It's his father's dying wish. And all paranormal sensations have ceased in the past couple of hours too, unless that's just the booze.

Joel holds onto the bannister as he makes his way, quietly, downstairs. He isn't sneaking. He's simply being careful because he's a little wasted, and he knows how the hardwood can be slippery in socks. June, and he's still wearing socks.

It sounds like a club down here, music and laughter coming from behind the swinging kitchen door. When he pushes it open a crack, it even looks like fun, because his wife is dancing at the sink, shaking that round, firm ass of hers, singing along to Michael Jackson.

Fun, until he sees Mike's eyes on Margo's backside. Fun, until Mike dances over with a dirty plate and puts his arms around her waist, with her still in front of him, and starts to wash it.

Before he knows it, Joel's pushed the door open, the sugar canister's in his hand, and he's taking aim.

Sara and I were a gang of two. Each other's moon. People rolled their eyes at us, called us snobby, stuck-up know-it-alls, and we didn't care a bit. We were geek girls, but with better wardrobes. We devoured the same books and movies, and people asked if we were sisters because we answered in tandem half the time. After a while, we started pretending it was true.

It was the fall of 1989. Eight months from then, high school— and the eighties—would be over. We thought we'd outlast it all.

||||||||||||||||||||||||||||||||

That October, we decided to endure the inane serfs that were our Grade 12 history classmates and go on the big field trip to the Boston area. Not because we wanted to look at bullet holes in old houses or walk through cemeteries, but because we could check out Harvard, take the tours, and get the T-shirts. We jumped at any reason to leave our small Ontario town, even if it meant bringing the locals with us.

On a Thursday afternoon, eight and a half hours after leaving home, our bus pulled into the parking lot of a Motel 6 in Boston and expelled us and twenty teenagers who'd been farting, belching, and burning through their Walkman batteries listening to "Like a Prayer" and "Funky Cold Medina" and eating Cheetos and peanut butter sandwiches. We were all ready to move: the jocks started wrestling, and the gym girls turned cartwheels on the asphalt while we waited for Mrs. Dobbs to check us in. Mr. Conway set into the jumping jacks and yelled at us to take part. Sara and I gave him the look—our withering best that we called just that, *the Wither*—and turned our backs and tried to think warmth into the pale, late afternoon sun.

When Sara was in the bathroom, someone came up behind me and covered my eyes with his hands. The hands were cold and slightly wet and smelled like Doritos.

"Guess who?" the person asked.

"Stop it, Scotty," I said. "I'm mad at you."

"About your wittle bunny?" He took his hands away from my face. Scott had stolen my grey Gund stuffed animal on the bus, and he and Greg—the two guys we were able to tolerate—had played football with it on the bus.

"That was a gift from my niece, okay? The one who died last year."

It was a lie, but I turned around and gave him the Wither. When the bunny came back to me, it smelled like Polo, Scotty and Greg's cologne. How very New England; Sara and I had taken turns snuggling with it, pretending it wasn't the fragrance we liked, just the coziness.

Scotty dropped his gaze to the ground. "Oops. Sorry, Lori."

"What's up with Conway?" I said.

Scotty laughed. "He's a gym teacher, remember?"

"What a knob."

Sara came out of the lobby holding a pamphlet about Salem. "This is where we're going tomorrow," she said. "Where all those witches were killed."

Scotty grabbed the brochure and stared at the back page. "Oooh," he said. "A haunted house."

Sara grabbed it back. "You're not scared of witches, are you?"

"Just of Dobbsy."

Everyone laughed. Scotty was nearly failing her Canadian history class.

"Looks more exciting than the battle sites," I said.

"Now, children," Scotty said, putting on Mrs. Dobbs's reedy voice and scrunching up his shoulders. "It's always exciting to see history where it was made."

"Kiss it," Greg said, and started walking on his hands.

He was always showing off like this. Still, both Sara and I couldn't help staring at his upside-down, perfectly balanced body. His shirt had fallen down over half his face, and we could see the dark vee of his chest hair, his nipples like mini peppermint patties.

"How special," Scotty said.

He left our little group, walked over to Mr. Conway, and started telling him a joke. Sara and I kept our eyes on Greg and his forearms. Greg kept his eyes on me.

||||||||||||||||||||||||||

A friendship is a strange and wonderful vehicle, able to transport the people within it to all kinds of new and exotic lands. It can also run out of gas, break down, trap you inside, burn oil, leave clouds of exhaust, tire tracks. Sara and me, we'd built that beast from the ground up, held it together with all the certainty and cynicism and ennui within us. The thing was a tank, meant to prevent anyone but us from boarding.

||||||||||||||||||||||||||

We were assigned a room with four other girls, a group of brun-
ettes we called the Fraud Squad because of their tendency to
shoplift. We unloaded our gear, claimed our beds—Sara and me
on the double, closest to the bathroom—and then obeyed the next
order to gather in the parking lot for a quick shopping trip before
dinner. While we waited for the whole group to assemble, and
Sara had run back to the room for her forgotten purse, Greg
decided to teach me how to spit.

"You have to move your whole body forward when you let it
go," Greg instructed.

"Propulsion, right? Increase the force behind the ammunition."

"Yeah, I guess. And keep your head up. Don't look down. You
want to get a nice big arc."

I gathered a ball of spit in my cheek and tried his technique.
It ended up on my chin and half a foot in front of me.

"Is that it?" he asked. "Is that all you can muster up?"

"I can't produce that much mucous on demand," I said, wiping
my face on my shoulder. "I need something to spit out."

He blushed first.

"Here," he said. He leaned down to pick a piece of grass from
beside the sidewalk. "Chew this."

I took it, inspected it for dirt, and stuck it in my mouth.

"Aaah!" he yelled. "Disgusting." Then he was laughing, holding
his stomach. "I can't believe you just did that."

"Grass is healthy. Chlorophyll, cellulose, fibre . . . . A billion
cows can't be wrong."

"What if I'd given you a worm? A billion robins might not be
wrong, either."

Sara returned, waving her purse in victory. I still had the grass
in my mouth. After I massed it into a ball, I let it fly.

"You're a fast learner," Greg said.

I waved at Sara. "Wanna try?"

She gave me a look that was nearly the Wither. Was I really
that far out of line?

Sara had never dated. Her parents were religious, so that was part of it, but frankly, she just didn't give off a welcoming vibe. Hair pulled severely into a ponytail, skin always a little red from swim club, not to mention the goggle marks, a rare smile that revealed a crooked front tooth; it didn't add up to your typical come-hither look. But she didn't seem to worry about it, and we never brought it up. Like I said, we were not living in the present. All of our attention was supposed to be on the horizon, from within our friendship, blind spots and all.

IIIIIIIIIIIIIIIIIIIIIIIIIIIIIIII

We shopped at hyper-speed when we finally got downtown. For the last twenty minutes of our little trip, Sara and I went to the Gap, a store we didn't have in Canada yet.

As we navigated the racks, I said, "I think Sir Scotty likes you."

"Oh, God."

"No, really."

She was quiet for a minute. "Do you think he's cute?"

"Sure," I said. "In a fetal kind of way. Hey, what do you think of this?" I was holding up a blue sweatshirt with a red logo. "Does Gap really mean 'gay and proud'?"

"*Fetal?*"

"You know. Unformed. Raw. I think it's his braces." They made his lower lip stick out so that you could see the inside of it, wet and pink.

"Better than the simian." She was talking about Greg, of course. She rifled through a rack of cargo pants, looking for ones with sale tags. "A guy his age shouldn't have that much hair."

"He can't help it," I said. "His father is Greek-Italian."

"Lori," she said, "do you actually like him?"

"I'm going to try this on." I lifted up a red sweater with wooden buttons.

"That looks like something my mother would wear."

"Really?" I held it up at both shoulders, squinting to see if I could see it. "It looks too old for me?"

"Maybe I'll buy one for her," Sara said. "Do they have it in green?"

"No," I said. "I'm just playing around with Greg. He's not even going to university. How could I ever think of him in that way?"

His father owned a landscaping business with a fleet of new trucks around town. He was being groomed for takeover.

In literature, what Sara and I came from was called humble beginnings. We wanted bigger. Better. To prove our focus on the future, I bought a blue Oxford dress shirt instead, a practical choice for a future career as lawyer, or doctor, or—we didn't know. The space beside "occupation" in our heads remained blank, but we knew it would be followed by some combination of initials, branding us with power.

||||||||||||||||||||||||||||||

The next day, after Paul Revere's house, an ancient graveyard, and a bunch of golden pineapples—the city's symbol of hospitality because whalers used to bring them back and set them by their doors to invite people in to eat exotic fruit—we set out for Salem.

We started our tour at Gallows Hill, where the people they called witches were massacred, all of them hanged except for one man who was pressed to death. The lesson I remember from that day, on how to do it: insert one man in between two slabs of rock, tie him down, add more rocks on top, and presto, two days later, one pressed human. The hangings seemed humane by comparison.

On our walk back down the hill to the Salem Witch Museum, the guide told us it had all happened in less than a year—hysterical youths claiming bewitchment, trials, verdicts, and executions.

It felt weird to be there, three hundred years later, traipsing down the path the condemned took on their way to the hanging site, making jokes, walking the other way as if it didn't matter in the least. Hysterical youths doing Scooby-Doo impressions.

Still, Sara and I paid attention to the crazy stuff we heard. Moles and birthmarks were called "witches' tits," a place for the Devil to suckle from a body. One scene in the museum murals depicted women being stuck with pins to see if their moles bled. If they didn't bleed, the women were obviously witches. Other murals showed clusters of pale-faced men in courtrooms and judges handing down the verdicts, sentencing people to be hanged.

"You have to understand the times they lived in," the guide said. "The small population had to stick together through hardship and disease. They just couldn't tolerate devil worship among them because that might mean a rift. United we stand, divided we fall, you know?"

One tableau depicted a woman named Tituba, the black slave of a minister, talking to Salem children and "warping" their pliant minds with talk of the Devil. Strangely, she was not one of the twenty-four people who died. She had confessed to practicing witchcraft and was allowed to leave town, unharmed. None of the dead had confessed.

"Oh, Tituba, you're breaking my heart," Scotty sang, to the tune of Simon and Garfunkel's "Cecilia."

"God, Scotty," I said. "Kind of crass, don't you think?"

He didn't stop. "Oh, Tituba, get down on your knees."

I watched Sara smile and then quickly hide it. "Let's leave these infants, Lori. Disgusting."

Twice every evening, the staff at the museum re-enacted the trial of an innocent woman, condemning her to death. We didn't get to see it, however, because the schedule said dinnertime.

After a repulsive meal at McDonald's, where some jerks started a ketchup fight and a blob landed on Sara's shirt like a nosebleed, we were given our tokens for the haunted house.

"You wanna skip this?" Greg asked me, out of earshot of the others. "Take a walk or something?"

Mrs. Dobbs and Mr. Conway had disappeared. "I don't know," I lied. "I kind of like a heart-stopping fright once in a while." My heart was nearly stopping with Greg's attention. But where was Sara? Weren't we supposed to go through the house together?

We walked a few paces before Greg clutched his chest. "Oh, God," he said. "I've been hit." He landed on the grassy boulevard and rolled onto his back, then gave one last gasp before his head lolled to the side.

"Nice try, there, Magnum PI." I nudged his leg with my shoe. He didn't move.

"Okay," I said. "See you later." I walked away, heart racing. He was back at my side within ten seconds.

"Hi there," he said, and draped his arm around my shoulder. "Let's do it. Let's get scared shitless."

I looked around for Sara. I was shaking. Where was she? But Sara wasn't going to help me through this one. No, it was better that she was somewhere else entirely. And where was Scotty?

"Oh, baby," I said, in my best eastern seaboard accent. "I thought you'd never ask."

||||||||||||||||||||||||||||||

The magazine promised a frightening experience. It didn't say terror. Greg and I walked past the bars of the first cage, and when a hand reached out for me, I screamed. Then I found my hand suddenly wrapped in another hand. I screamed louder until I realized it was Greg's.

"It's okay," he said. Greg kept holding my hand. I could feel the calluses on his palms from where he held shovels and rakes. Another creature jumped out at us. I screamed again and squeezed Greg's hand. He squeezed back.

My arms had goosebumps. I knew it was physiological, a common reaction to being creeped out, but it wasn't only that: I was holding hands with a boy who shaved every morning.

"Aren't you scared?" I asked him.

He leaned down so his lips were grazing my ear. The whole right side of my body got gooseflesh. "Yes," he said. "Isn't that the point?"

We made it out of the haunted house with only a few more screaming episodes. Then Greg led me to a stand of trees along Salem Commons, pulled me closer, and planted a kiss on my lips.

A kiss. This kiss. It was not in the long-term plans. Not in the curriculum. But I remember it now as clearly as if I'd been studying it for years: the sureness of his mouth on mine, the warmth. I hadn't really dated either, but I'd played around a bit. The other boys I'd kissed before, who numbered exactly two, had been tentative, nervous, their kisses leading to nothing but a string of slow dances in the gym. I kissed him back. He tasted like Pepsi and Big Red cinnamon gum.

"Um," I said. "Should we be doing this here?"

"You're right," Greg said. "Let's go somewhere else."

"Won't they be looking for us?" How much time did we have? I'd lost all sense of it.

"Nah, we've still got loads of time." He leaned in closer to my ear. "Let's go see if the bus is open," he whispered. "Just for a few minutes."

"Dobbs will lose it."

"She doesn't have to know a thing."

How had Greg known? The bus driver was nowhere to be seen, but he had left the doors open. We climbed the stairs and checked every seat as we walked the aisle: no one else on board.

"What if we get caught?" I said.

Greg laughed. "Relax." He shifted his hands down my back until they were on my bum. "You have an amazing ass," he said into my hair.

I'd never even thought of it as an ass before. He grabbed my bum harder this time, as if the cheeks were apples he might break in half with his bare hands, something I'd seen him do in the cafeteria.

"We should go," I said. But did I mean it? Why did it matter what his father did, or what he did after Grade 12, or whether we wanted the same things in the future? I was shaking. I wanted more kisses. Wanted more.

He slid his hand under my shirt, fingers climbing to the lace of my bra. My nipples reacted as they were programmed to do, standing up straight and tall and ready for more of the same. I gasped a little as we sank to the seat. He unbuttoned my shirt and ran his tongue over the mole on my shoulder. I could feel him murmuring against my skin.

"What was that?" I pulled away to hear him better.

"You're a witch."

"Are you afraid?"

He laughed. "Oh, yeah. The Devil's gotten inside of you," he said. "But I know how to get him out."

He had just wedged his other hand between my legs, pressing up gently into my crotch while my hand found his waistband, when we heard people entering the bus. Greg quickly pulled me down to lie beside him.

"You see anyone?" Sara's voice said.

"Nah," Scotty's voice said. "But it was worth a shot."

Greg covered my mouth with his palm and guided one of my hands to the front of his jeans.

"Shit," Sara said. "If they don't show soon, they're going to get it. I don't know what's gotten into Lori."

"Yeah, well," Scotty said. "Greg's had a crush on her forever."

Greg pressed his palm harder against my lips. I pressed my hand against the shape of his penis. His breath caught, his heart drumming against my shoulder. I bit Greg's palm, lightly. He put his other hand back between my legs, and I bit harder. There were maybe five seconds before we were about to be found, but my body, and his body, they didn't care. We would go down burning.

Sara sighed loudly. I knew that sound well: she was pissed off. "I guess we better keep looking."

"I guess," Scotty said. "Unless you want to just hang out here?"

"Nah, I don't think so," she said. "We've spent way too much time on this bus."

We heard two sets of footsteps leave the bus. Alone again.

IIIIIIIIIIIIIIIIIIIIIIIIIIII

When the teachers and the rest of the class came back on board, Greg and I pretended that we were in the right, that we'd followed instructions to meet on the bus. For some reason, they believed us.

Sara completely ignored me the whole ride back to the hotel. She sat with Scotty, though, so that was a good sign.

Once we got back, we got the warning.

"Big day, tomorrow, guys," Mr. Conway told us. "No foolin' around tonight." He looked pointedly at me, then Greg, before heading into his room.

Greg popped into another handstand in the hallway, waving with his feet.

"Show off," Sara muttered. "Ta-ta for now," she said, louder. Scotty was walking backwards and nearly bumped his head on the vending machine. Still trying to impress her.

Mrs. Dobbs popped her head in at ten o'clock and delivered the half-hour warning. Then I watched through the peephole as she doubled back to Mr. Conway's room, running her talons through her frizzy hair.

Sara wouldn't say a word to me. We went to sleep in the same bed, under the same covers, but it was like I was dead to her.

||||||||||||||||||||||||||||||||

We spent the whole next day at Harvard, Sara and I as far from each other as possible. Twice, when no one was looking, Greg pulled me aside and kissed me.

After our tour and souvenir shopping, the bus took us back to the hotel, and in a moment of lax judgement, Mr. Conway allowed us all another half-hour of free time before we were to meet for dinner at a seafood restaurant across the highway. Once the Fraud Squad was enmeshed in a game of euchre in the courtyard, I pulled out the Pearl Drops teeth-whitening kit we'd bought at a drugstore downtown.

"Give it a try with me?" I asked. I'd never felt that alone before. It was a freeze-out.

She put down her eyeliner and looked at my mouth. "Yeah, you could use it."

I took it as a step in the right direction.

The box said it would only take half an hour, but by the time we got the stuff plastered onto our yellowed canines, it was time to go. Scotty and Greg came knocking on our door. We ignored them. Then Mrs. Dobbs. I told her we had a bit of girl trouble, and that we'd come as soon as we could.

While chemicals stripped our enamel, we did our makeup, tidied our suitcases, flipped through tourist magazines. Anything to avoid talking.

"This place was crazy." I pointed at a picture of the haunted house we'd been in. It was hard to talk with the whitener on, but I tried my best. "Were you not scared out of your mind in there?"

"No, I knew what was coming," Sara said with her pasty mouth.

"I'm a sucker." It was true. I got scared watching teen flicks intended to scare kids exactly like me.

"Schucker," Sara said, foaming a little at the lips.

"All day schucker," I said. "All day."

At least that got a half-smile out of her.

After the thirty minutes were fully up, we rinsed and finished our prep for dinner, admiring the shine of our teeth every few seconds. Sara let her hair down like she was ready for bed, a hump in the back of it from her scrunchie, and paired it with her red Gap rugby shirt. I added a bit more mousse to my hair and wore my new blue Oxford, the one Greg had unbuttoned.

Ready.

We raced each other the half-block to the highway, with me ahead by a centimetre.

"I'm starving," Sara complained when we got to the highway. "I don't want to walk all the way down there and back." She pointed at the walkway, arching over the road three hundred metres down. The restaurant was directly across from us.

"But wasn't it worth it?" I asked, pointing to my mouth. "One must suffer to be beautiful."

"Come on," she said. "Let's make a run for it."

"No way," I said, but I followed her to stand beside the four huge signs telling us to USE WALKWAY.

She watched the traffic.

"This is crazy," I said. "They're all coming way too fast."

"We can do it," she said. She looked like she was waiting for the right time to jump in for Double Dutch. There never seemed to be a right time. Then, she must've noticed a space in the stream of lights because before I knew it, she'd grabbed my arm and pulled me across five eastbound lanes.

Ten or twenty horns blared at us, a chorus of angry bleats and wails, but we'd made it to the traffic divider, with another five-lane stream to cross.

"You almost got us killed!" I screamed.

"No, I didn't! Anyway, we're halfway to dinner now."

"Jesus, Sara. What's the matter with you?"

"With me? What's the matter with me? How about you, all over Mr. Hot Stuff like a . . . like a . . . whore!"

"What are you talking about?" I could feel my whole body trembling. "We just about died, and you're calling me a whore?"

"Did you do it with him, Lori?" She stood in front of me, arms across her chest. "Did you?"

I jumped when another car laid on the horn as it screamed past us. I didn't know what she counted as *it*. He hadn't come inside me, but stars had exploded. We'd made plans to sneak out later that night. I shook my head.

"I don't believe you." She turned away from me; she was crying. "I thought we had a deal!"

"I know! And I'm still in!"

We both stood there, looking at the restaurant across the road where our classmates were probably filling up on free bread or crackers while they waited.

The traffic between us and them was lighter, but neither of us was making a run for it.

"Sara," I called. "Come on. Please. What's the big deal? I fooled around with Greg. It's not like we're getting married!"

"I know that! But still." Still crying, she bit her lip. Lips that hadn't, as far as I knew, ever touched another mouth.

She walked away from me, but she couldn't go far: there was nowhere to go. She just stood there and stared at the traffic, hugging herself.

"Halfway there." I held out my hand. "Let's go."

"See ya." Sara sat down on a concrete barrier. Her long hair blew into her face. She wouldn't look at me, not even to give me the Wither.

"They're waiting for us. We've gotta go. Come on, Sara! You brought me this far, now let's just get there."

"I'm not coming with you."

I waited for her to change her mind, but then the traffic slowed right down. My window of opportunity. "I'm going," I called out. "I'm going now!"

From inside the restaurant, where I sat between Greg and Scotty, I couldn't even see her.

Gerry was barely two years old the day her mother painted the
BARKERS' BERRIES sign for the main road, just before their
first decent crop had ripened. Eighteen years later, the memory of
that sign was as fresh as this morning's breakfast, although *that*
hadn't been fresh at all—a stale bagel, toasted and smeared with
the last of her peanut butter.

Her mother was the artist in the family, and the smiling
strawberry being carted in a wagon was far beneath her abil-
ities, as if Chagall had been asked to design a business card for
a daycare. But she hadn't minded a bit, at least not in Gerry's
memory; it meant her work would be seen beyond the high-school
notebooks she kept in a damp box in the basement. It would be
seen thousands of times a week, in fact, to entice people driving
by to come down their long laneway to buy their berries, and
later, when the business had grown enough to sponsor the local
team, on T-shirts and Tyke hockey jerseys.

Gerry and her five-year-old sister Patti were no help at all that
day; their mother needed her full attention for the graphic design
job. So, she'd set them in their empty kiddie pool with a whole bag
of mini marshmallows and told them to stay put. The sun went

higher, the day grew hot, and although they were within sight, their mother didn't notice what they'd been doing until Gerry began to cry.

"Can't see! Can't see!" she wailed, and then only cried louder after Patti dumped a pail of water on her head.

Their mother came running, and when she saw Gerry, began to roar with laughter, which brought their father out from the closest barn.

Gerry had stuck her eyes completely closed with marshmallow goo.

"What's all this?" he said. Then he, too, had a good chuckle at Gerry's expense before lifting the screaming toddler up and away for a bath.

She didn't really know if this was a first memory or just a story retold so often it had become embedded in her brain, but Gerry held onto this moment as a pure one, a portrait of a young family, early summer, a moment she crawled back into when there was nowhere else as golden.

IIIIIIIIIIIIIIIIIIIIIIIIIIIIII

Some days, Gerry felt the sky press down on her like a pillow to her face, a diagnosis, a death. But she was young and privileged and healthy—as far as she knew. It didn't matter. After months of Vancouver Island rain, she had reached her limit. She'd been warned, on the train trip west and often since then, about the winters, but just as often, people had consoled her with statistics about the mainland being worse. Thirty percent less rain here! Far fewer suicides! Did she look that sad?

Her roommate, Flora, called Gerry's emerald-green shirt "a gift to the eyes" when she saw it after a long shift at the at-risk youth health clinic. Many things were gifts: the weather, a day off, her meditation teacher. Other reminders she was no longer in rural Ontario? The rainbow crosswalk. Artisanal doughnuts. Lavender cakes. The bearded, beaded guy in a sarong who served her coffee. The fruitiness of the coffee beans, not roasted until black and oily but just to the colour of her hair—chestnut. The chestnuts littering the streets last autumn like giant June bugs. Trees taller than the highest buildings in the city, or so it seemed from the ground.

If she wrote it all down in an email to her sister, as she longed to, it would seem fictitious, fanciful, farcical. She could just hear her replies too: who cared about the name of the family who grew her coffee beans, or if drug addicts had safe places to shoot up? But Gerry hadn't contacted Patti in weeks, not since Christmas, and even then, it had just been a few texts back and forth, a couple seasonal emojis, a photo of her nephew in a storm of wrapping paper, not even looking at the camera. Her mother and father had wished her Merry Christmas on the phone, but they'd mailed no gifts, just a card with a fifty-dollar bill tucked inside. Gerry had sent them a package of smoked salmon, wrapped in paper embedded with wildflower seeds, to be planted in the spring.

Tonight, Gerry was at the Norway House for the Sunday Night Folk Music series. It was partly a reward for making it through the winter, and partly a huge challenge she'd set for herself: to perform at an open stage. She'd been playing guitar for a few years, writing songs for less than that, singing since before she could talk, but the only times she'd officially performed had been at the church hall Christmas concert and once in the high-school talent show, when she'd played "Blowin' in the Wind." The boys in the smoke pit had gotten good mileage out of that one, for months teasing her every time she walked past to get to the buses waiting out behind the school.

"Limit's three, if you get on," the woman in charge explained. She was draped in various layers of beige, like a tree wrapped up against the winter. "But we like newbies, so you'll get on for sure."

The woman must've seen fear on Gerry's face, to flash her that candy necklace of a smile. "Now go get yourself a cup of tea and a cookie. There are at least five people up before I'll call on you."

She did as she was told and took her tea and cookie to a chair along the wall, standing her battered guitar case up beside her. The room was filled with couples in matching fleecewear and single oldsters with bowed heads, likely more from the weight of them than reverence, although it was hard to tell the difference. She knew no one.

She felt the urge to do the one thing she had done for most of her life, which was to tuck her long single braid beneath her bum and sit on it. But she'd cut her hair when she left home. It was still far from short, but if she let it loose, its ends met her shoulders like the fringed and tickling legs of a millipede. Mostly it was ponytailed or flipped further, as it was now, into an elastic-band bun. The ghost of her long hair ached like a missing limb.

There was a religious hint in the air; the low, reverent light, the unamplified musicians saying gentle things not everyone could hear. The air smelled like coffee and ginger tea, and cheeks were rosy, wrinkled, no strangers to folk fest sun. A saggy goodness seemed to hold the building up; it was a wooden balloon, and all the conversations people might have had at church years ago were happening here, tonight, out of the mouths of the Gore-Texed and the denimed, a melodious rumble that made Gerry feel both particularly welcome and extremely sad.

Every person had their heart facing the stage, open, receiving, except there was no leader, no cross to look to—only a couple of framed royals on either side of the stage, Queen Elizabeth and Prince Philip separated by the stage. But oh, the guitar sounds coming from the man currently onstage! A tangled, woven, multi-coloured offering, like stained glass turned to filament.

Three songs. What would she choose? Should she warm them up with a cover, move into a little original, end with another cover? A sandwich. An original sandwich.

There was more plaid in the folk house than she'd seen in all her months in this city, combined. The word *fellowship* surfaced in Gerry's mind, and she knew it had been hovering there ever since she left the farm—the need she could not name. Gerry was at home here, and as far from it as she'd ever been. Her identity was cracking, shifting, reforming like river ice.

Her hand trembled on her pebbled leather guitar case. Would she dare? Maybe she wasn't scared; maybe her fingers were just picking up the vibrations of the music on stage.

The songs people were playing were all about love, it seemed, whether for people or the land, and Gerry's chest felt like a knuckle church, folding into itself. She'd never been in love, not in the romantic sense of it, anyway. What would she play? She knew some Dylan. "Tangled Up in Blue," done slowly, and "Blowin' in the Wind," of course. It would be best to keep it simple; this audience was here to sing, to take part, to support. And who was she kidding? This was her first real gig. *Hello, my name is Gerry, and I am a folksinger. Hello, Gerry.* Simple would be perfectly fine.

An older couple had come onstage and were singing "Goodnight, Irene," and she was catapulted back home, to the kitchen, her father shaving by the sink, with his bowl and brush and straight razor, the AM radio wailing out the sadness. It was the first thing she pictured when she thought of him. Why? It was the only time he was relatively still, aside from his hands; she got the sense that he was enjoying himself, and he seemed to be in a better mood once he was done. Or was it that Gerry never saw him like this, in his undershirt, except while shaving? A vulnerability, an intimacy that made her feel tight inside, a fear and a thrill. Nothing sexual, not that kind of intimate, but a sense that he was soft inside, like everyone else—something she rarely glimpsed.

Farming had an intimacy, but it was the intimacy of hands clapping. Contact, pressure, sound, and yet little awareness of skin or connection in the more cosmic sense. Yet farming wasn't cosmic. A person had jobs to do, she did them.

According to her father, Gerry was not farming material. She had the build for it, sure, but she was impractical, as soft as homemade ice cream. He was right. All she wanted to do on the land was to take her horse out to the far fields on the pretense of checking livestock. Once there, if the conditions were right, she'd dismount and unsaddle him, then let him gallop free, nothing to impede his natural instinct, no one making him do anything he didn't want to do.

‖‖‖‖‖‖‖‖‖‖‖‖‖‖‖‖‖‖‖‖‖‖‖‖‖‖

Her mother had begun to get sick when Gerry was about ten, after having a miscarriage, and had progressively worsened. It looked, from the outside, like that had been the initial push, the instigating factor, the bit of sand in the pearl.

Gerry read the health magazine headlines in Victoria, the commands to stop inflammation by saying no to nightshades, coffee, sugar, grains, non-organic produce, red meat. But she knew her mother wouldn't go for any of this. No, if there had been a window of time in which anything could save her, she believed it was closed now, bricked over, about to be sealed with a head-stone—already chosen, in fact, for the family plot. No amount of quinoa could save her.

She'd gotten much worse in Gerry's last year of high school, which is why she was here on the coast; her grades had dropped too low to get into university, and so, she'd worked at a small café until she'd saved enough to come west for a general arts diploma at a community college.

There were tests available to see if she had the markers of this disease, but Gerry didn't want to take them. A part of her still couldn't believe that someone could get this ill from arth-ritis and possibly die. It was like getting gangrene from a paper cut. But the ghost of possibility hung around her, along with her cut-off braid; every sensation in her joints sent a jolt of fear through her, and any other pain too. Her mother was nearing organ failure—the rheumatoid arthritis unable to stay put in the joints, spreading, diving deep into lungs and heart and eyes, so that in the end she would most likely be blind and starving, unable to breathe.

Her mother wasn't the only one who'd suffered. A few years back, Gerry's sister, Patti, had been diagnosed with thyroid problems. She was twenty-two at the time, and already a mother to little Joe, married at twenty to a guy named Rick whom she'd dated since Grade 11. The problem soon grew to have another name—cancer—and within weeks Patti was radioactive, her throat shot through with beams of destruction. Bam! Kill the killer.

Gerry had stepped in to help take care of Joe, who was barely walking, barely talking, and at times inconsolable without his mama and her milk. Once, she tried bringing him to the hospital to see Patti, but all they could do was stare and wave and cry through inch-thick glass. Every bodily fluid was a danger.

Now Patti, a puffier and less energetic version of herself, was clear of the cancer, and Joe had just started kindergarten, and Gerry ached to see them. But she'd put two and two together and could come up with only one reason that both her mother and sister had gotten ill in the first place: the farm itself. She hadn't come this far west just for college or because she was a terrible nurse and that was a likely path for her if she'd stayed home—caretaking her mother—but because she was trying to stay safe.

Her father had stopped talking to her; it had been three months, and other than a strained Merry Christmas, there had been only silence. Each day, she willed her phone to ring, with his voice on the other end. Three months ago, she'd told him about the evidence she'd been gathering about pesticides and hormone-based cancers and autoimmune diseases, and he had done what she'd been afraid of: he'd seen it as blame. And who wouldn't? Who wouldn't feel like she'd just backhoed a bucketful of cow manure right onto his head, a shitload of guilt he was supposed to assume? Her mother couldn't talk for long when she was occasionally able to reach her on the phone; her voice was weak, and she only talked about the weather, how cold, how stormy, how hard her father was working.

Plenty of the soil on her family's farm was rich, and it had provided full, diverse crops for a very long time: crops eaten in season and put up in jars for the long winters that followed. But somewhere along the way, someone had gotten ambitious. Her father's father was the one who suggested his son clear another acre or two and put in potatoes to sell. Then, where the soil was largely clay, someone had come up with the idea of strawberries as a cash crop because of the sun exposure, and Barkers' Berries was born. Much doctoring came afterwards, fixing up the pH, making those tooth-leafed plants take hold. But after all this trouble, more trouble followed. Pests, wind, and nastier weather—and the chemical fixes that matched. Strawberries were a volatile crop; they were prone to mildew, root rot, sun scald, slime mould, leaf spot, and injury from frost, just to name the common blights— never mind the pests like aphids, slugs, and weevils or how they needed to be picked every couple of days from their back-breaking, low-growing rows. And the birds! How many scarecrows had she and Patti made to help protect the berries?

Gerry didn't blame her father for trying to make the farm yield more returns. They'd had a few good years, with gorgeous berries renowned throughout the county for their sweetness, their size. She blamed his methods and the world they were living in and how far they'd strayed from loving the land her ancestors had come to one hundred and fifty years ago with only hope and muscle.

Tonight she could see his posture in some of the men in the folk club, broad shoulders beginning to migrate forward, hair gone to white or silver. The man beside her had big, rough-looking hands resting on his lap, on well-worn jeans, and what looked like a gravy stain on his blue button-up shirt—an older version of her father. Her father, who'd had to give up most of the farming and get a shiftwork job at the 3M plant for the benefit plan and a steady income. She missed him so much—and the rest of the family too—that it felt like knives in her throat.

IIIIIIIIIIIIIIIIIIIIIIIIIIIIII

The crowd was applauding, now, for the couple in matching cowboy shirts who'd played Gordon Lightfoot's "If You Could Read My Mind" after "Goodnight, Irene" and "Red River Valley." Was she folk enough to be at this venue?

After a heartfelt round of applause, a woman in a black one-piece fleece jumpsuit got up to make the weekly announcements. The headlining trio, younger and cooler than Gerry had expected, had come in during the last song, their shoulders speckled with petals—cherry blossoms were covering the city in pink snow. She had heard this band on the radio; it had won a CBC contest for a song about the coast.

Now two of the three men were talking quietly, back near the concession, and a hobbled older guy in a blanket coat got up to shush them. The musicians looked around for support, laughing silently, surprise on their faces at being scolded, and found Gerry looking back at them. She smiled conspiratorially, then felt her face burn. She pulled her eyes away and scraped at the edge of her guitar case, at a mark that wasn't there.

What Gerry wanted to sing, suddenly, was "Kumbaya." She felt like it might, somehow, be a big enough song to travel across four provinces. To her sister, who didn't know what to make of all the information Gerry had sent; to her mother, who cried for hours a day over the rifts, physical and emotional; and to her father, who, whenever he lit their bonfires, used to sing this song in jest, mocking all who would do so for real. But still, he'd always sung it so beautifully, shaking up the calm night air with his antler-velvet voice.

She had never been lonely before. That was the truth of it hitting her here, right now. She'd done the leaving, the bridge-burning, but it didn't matter who'd done what. She was bereft, alone. Being in the room just brought it on more acutely, the way shaking after a trauma only begins once it's safe enough to let go—in the presence of what you need most. Her sister knew this: during her recovery, Gerry had heard her say things like, "Don't you dare say one nice thing to me, or I will lose it." *It* being her cool—steel in the face of steel was her method of holding herself together.

But art didn't come from that—and she was getting up on that stage soon. Could she hold it together, or would a Joni Mitchell cover make her break down?

There was no one checking in on her, seeing how she was. That was the worst of the loneliness, worse than the missing them. Not to be missed.

The question she'd been carrying with her, and ignoring, was this: what would happen next? If someone told her the news, long distance, that her mother had passed away, what would she do then? The running from what couldn't be changed was nothing more than foolish, like a hide-and-seek game when the hider closed her eyes and was convinced that the seeker couldn't see her.

Maybe not soon, but Gerry's mother was going to die. Everyone was. And Gerry was so far away, protesting. A lot of good that was doing anyone. And what would she be left with? A plate, a cup, a vase? Her mother's old navy and white swimsuit, the belt of it she clung to all those years ago, afraid to float until she let go?

The year Gerry had learned to swim, when she was seven or eight, she'd had to let go, to soften, to pretend to not be afraid. Her mother was teaching her in the village, at the park on the river, and she took her and Patti there at least once a week that summer. Patti was gone as soon as they got there, swimming and playing with her friends from school, an easy banter among them that made Gerry jealous. Her mother back then was strong and tanned, comfortable in her body, and more patient than she usually was as Gerry clung to her, unwilling to let go entirely. But eventually, one August day, her mother told her that they were just going to float. "Pretend your arms and legs and head are made of marshmallows," she said. "No bones, no muscles. Now put your marshmallow self to bed on the water. Just lie down like it's your bed. Don't kick!" she reminded her. "Just let yourself sink into bed." For some reason, Gerry did what she was told, and she relaxed enough to let herself float on that river, silky, black, and slow.

And now, she was up. The draped woman had just announced her—"Ge-rry from Ontari-O"—and Gerry's legs carried her to the front of the room, past the single seated men along the outer wall, past the elderly couples, the long-haired, and the other new performer, John, from New Brunswick, who'd been eager as a border collie.

The others had all said a few words to introduce their performances. Gerry just wanted to play and then sit down again.

But she stood in front and forced herself to look out at the audience, and the trick her sister had given her, way back in elementary school, came back: find one person out there who could act as a mirror, so that it would just seem like she was practising at home, alone.

When Gerry looked out, she found a dozen mirrors, maybe twenty, a roomful of hearts all willing her to play, already loving it. *Soften, Gerry*, she told herself. *Let go. Float.*

"Hi there," she said. "I'm Gerry."

"A little louder, honey," someone called from the back.

"Okay." She dove in. "Hi. I took the train out here from back east because I wanted to see the country from the ground.

Leaving home for the first time, it's not easy. And when I was on that train, I felt as if I could see ghosts. People who'd made the same journey, before the railway, on horseback or by wagon. When the country was young and the land was pure. I wrote this song on the train. It's called 'Missing What I Never Had.'"

The covers could wait. She played her song, stumbling only once on the bar chords, only playing the cheater F chord a couple of times, and at the end, there was applause, and even a little cheering—was it coming from the headliners, maybe that cute bass player? Who else would whistle like they were at a rock concert?

Gerry then moved into Joni's "Both Sides Now" and followed it with "Kumbaya" because this audience wanted to sing along. And yes, she cried a little, but held herself together until the end.

She hadn't bombed. She took her bow to lots of clapping, then quickly left the stage with her guitar and found her case along the side wall while the woman in beige introduced the last performer before the break and the main act.

Then she felt a tap on her shoulder.

"Hey, good set," the band's bass player said. "I love what you did with the Mitchell song."

She blushed, deeply. "Thank you. I, uh, love your music too."

"You've heard us before?"

"On the radio."

The bass player laughed. "Good ol' CBC. Well, thank you very much. Come up and get a CD after the show."

"Wow, thank you," she said. "And break a leg." Was that okay, to say that to a musician, or was it only for actors?

He winked at her before returning to his bandmates.

Gerry sat down to listen to the last act, a teenage boy with long hair, playing an Elvis song on the ukulele, and playing it well. She pulled her phone from her pocket—a habit she was trying to break—just to chill herself out. Her performance had been more of a rush than she could have imagined.

She'd done it! She'd played onstage. And the bass player had just winked at her.

There was a text waiting for her, from Patti.

> Mom wanted you to see this.

She'd sent a photo of an old snapshot that Gerry knew well: the four of them on the front porch of their big old farmhouse, all tanned, young, and smiling, Gerry in their mother's lap, Patti in their father's. Their grandma's big yellow mixing bowl sat between them, heaped full of strawberries.

Then Patti sent a photo of the back of it too.

FIRST HARVEST was written in faded ballpoint pen. And, below it, in fresher ink, but shakier writing: WE MISS YOU.

Gerry wiped her eyes with her sleeve.

The ukulele player left the stage after just one song, and the audience was on the move, heading toward her and the concession. She couldn't face them or the nice things they might say, not right now. Quickly she made a beeline for the door and out into the blustery evening. A few smokers had beaten her to the door, and she faked a conversation on her phone as she passed them, smiling.

She texted Patti from the sidewalk.

> Thank you. Is Mom still awake, do you think? For a chat?

The band would need at least ten minutes to set up, which meant she had time to call home, but it was after eleven there. Well past bedtime, especially for her father, if he was on day shifts. But Patti had just sent the photo. Maybe she'd just been there?

Patti texted right back.

> She's up. The new drug she's on gives her insomnia. Good thing it's working otherwise. She held a paintbrush last week!!!

A paintbrush.

It had been years since her mother could hold anything besides a Kleenex.

Gerry texted back.

That's amazing news. Calling now. xoxo.

When her mother answered, her voice was stronger, well beyond the whisper it had been at Christmas.

"Barkers'," she said, as if the farm was still running, and it wasn't the middle of winter, and she wasn't sick, and Gerry was a customer, wanting to know when their beautiful berries would be ready.

That's his map of the world. Above the fireplace.

I don't see the wonders. I just don't see them. Mind you, I don't lie on the living room floor like he did, staring at the thing, imagining the adventures we'd have. There's no carpet anymore, so where would I even lie? Not that I would've—God, dust mites are one of the worst allergens. I feel itchy just thinking about it.

He wanted the rug when he left, but I put my foot down, since I'm the one who chose it to match the couch. I guess I could've had him make me an offer, instead of the crazy girl from Craigslist who came on a scooter. She strapped the thing right onto her seat and then just rode away on it, broomstick-style, waving. I nearly died from worrying I'd caused an accident.

No, what I see when I look at that map is clutter. I want to tidy it up, join the gaudy chunks of land, put them back where they belong. My eyes can't seem to help it. Humans have to fit things together: hand and hand, tongue and tooth, man-parts into female, or otherwise. It's natural.

My living room is a mess because of the world.

I wonder about the why of it, sometimes, all that distance between the land masses. And despite its faux-antique look—the oceans are not blue but brown up there, a kind of fake parchment, his idea of posh—it reminds me of Grade 6 homework, the endless shading of provinces or the patchy countries of Africa. The teacher probably told us why the earth looks the way it does too, but why would I remember that? I'm no geographer, if that's even a word. Ugh. I hate ugly words.

The thing is, no matter how hard I squint to keep the pieces together, they float apart again. I'd stitch them together if I could. Of course, I'd have to use the strongest thing in the world. Hemp? It's not just for smoking. But no. It'd have to be on an epic scale. Dinosaur skin, that kind of thing. As if that's going to be easy to find. All we have left are their bones made into oil, and they're all nearly burnt up.

But what if I could manage, by some miracle, to lasso the continents together? It'd ease transportation costs to Europe. I wouldn't mind the Italian shoes being closer—my calves really do feel better in soft, dreamy boots from the Boot. My muscles can contract more easily. It's natural, since we've been wearing animal skins forever, and God, that fake stuff? It cracks after about three days.

I guess it might bring people closer too, you know, like one big party. Unity, oneness, what they rave about at church and such.

I've tried it. I lived with other people, way before he moved in, and the idea seemed noble enough. But I know what it feels like to have someone eat your whole pint of Häagen-Dazs or drink your last beer. I know what it's like to have a roommate yelling for more, you know, *lovin'*, and getting it.

All things being equal, well, nothing ever is. If Africa huddled up against the Atlantic States, would peace prevail? Would the reptiles of Madagascar play nicely with Australian kangaroos? Would Newfoundlanders start taking two-hour lunches and wearing matching panties and bras once they were spooning with France? And what would happen to our good highways, our farms and fruit trees, our empty shopping malls? Would the party be worth the hangover?

I should take the stupid map down. I happen to know, however, that it's covering the hole he put in the wall from trying to hang that heavy mirror of his. I didn't want it there, but oh no, he had to try, said it was meant to hang over the fireplace as a centrepiece. I don't want to look at myself like that all the time. I'm not ugly—I've gone to therapy, I've worked that stuff out—but isn't art a better choice for a focal point? Doesn't a mirror as the centre of attention make you seem kind of vain? While he struggled to hang the mirror, I told him about the time I lived in Germany, on an exchange programme, in a home with no mirrors at all. How I only had my compact, and how it made me feel the best I've ever felt about myself, not being able to see the whole picture at once. He tilted his head, all thoughtful and considerate, and then just said, help me hold this up, will you?

I didn't tell him that I went to a friend's house every chance I had to make sure I wasn't sprouting bulges or wings or that, after a few days, I started to feel like my body was made up of bits and pieces, like I might break apart into islands of limbs and torso and head. I didn't feel whole.

Feelings. Now there's something strong. If I could harness those and pull the continents together, then I'd have a chance. Like the first time I fell in love. That's powerful. Best drug ever. And no, it wasn't with him, although I never brought that up. He wanted to be a pioneer, touching new ground. Ha.

Then there's sensation: if I stroke my inner thigh, right now, well, that's bigger than any thought. Or rub the end of my nose or pull on my hair five times like I do before a conversation. Those are gigantic. Powerful.

But not to him—he never supported my diagnosis. Thought it was a weakness, taking meds, like I could overcome my anxiety disorder if I just did the homework. Like if he lined up the shoes in height order for me, everything would go back into place, and I'd be someone he could love more completely. It doesn't work that way, I kept telling him. I have to line things up myself.

And even if I line up the shoes just right, on my own, it only helps for a minute.

Anxiety dis-order. Ha, that's a good one. Even the name is messy.

I bet, though, if I could truly make those continents join up, I might feel better. And wouldn't my name go down in history! The woman who stitched the world back together. It'd be a comfort, knowing my name would live on after I'm dead. What a lovely thought.

Of course, if I could solve that little inconvenience—dying— well, then, I'd never be forgotten. Everyone living, everyone not born yet, they'd all worship me. Forget reuniting the continents, how about eternal life?

Just one problem that I can see.

That's going to be too many people, making more babies, more garbage, more gadgets, more bad music, more lineups. More clutter.

Back to the map.

I have to do something to make it work. I might have to get my old Laurentien pencil crayons out again and sharpen them all to dangerous points; just pick a colour and start at one end, make a tidal wave of such intensity that it would swallow the whole world.

I just wish I had something else to hang on the wall. Something to pick up the orange and blue flecks of the uphol- stery. I like things to coordinate. He didn't match me, that was all. When I threw him out—he'll tell you different, but it was me, telling him to go—he was wearing unmatched socks when he put on his shoes. And one of them was mine! If I'd had any misgivings, they vanished the moment he took his slippers off.

But still, the place is pretty dismal now. That rug did lend a certain coziness to the room, even with its microscopic organisms. And I do miss the way he used to come up from behind and hug me, without turning me around. I don't think it was because he didn't want to see my face.

We were South America and Africa, though, places you couldn't imagine being one. In my perfect world, however, they'd go back to being attached to—well, you already know.

Yes. I'll start with the ocean. Brown just won't do. When I'm done colouring it tonight, it'll match the couch. If he doesn't call, wanting to see a movie. If he doesn't want to talk about his day or say he's sorry for yelling at me when I couldn't stop checking to see if the door was locked. He needed his sleep, I get it. I just can't help myself.

Better yet, I'll cut the continents out, nestle them together into one big island. If I paint the whole wall blue, I could float my new world on it, wherever I want.

Now that would be a beautiful thing.

What a prodigious growth this English Race,
especially the American Branch of it is having!
How soon will it subdue and occupy all the
wild parts of this continent and of the islands
adjacent. No prophecy, however seemingly
extravagant, as to future achievements in this
way are likely to equal the reality.

—Rutherford Hayes, 1856
19th president of the USA, 1877–1881

We don't like to brag. We label bragging as a slight toxin in the system, a habit we've been working on purging since we got here.

Hmm. Let me rephrase that. *Got here* implies owning the place. To *get it* implies striving. We are not keen on these kinds of verbs. No. When we *arrived*, I meant to say. When we *merged* with this paradise, where all our dreams have been made real.

No, we don't mean to brag, but we can't really help it. This afternoon Don and I have been driving around our island, and

I know we're both entertaining the thought that free-floats in our heads pretty much 24/7, something we give airtime to when we just can't hold it back: this place is freaking amazing. It's awesome! Incredible! Too good to be true!

But then we make our faces go soft and placid again; we summon peace and wonder, invoke calmness to descend like warm water from our solar shower. It is true, and believable, because we, Holly and Don Russell, are living proof that dreams and dreamscapes can all manifest in real time. You can live your perfect amazing life, and no one can stop you or SO HELP THEM!

Just joking! Violence is not allowed here. Well, *allowed* isn't exactly right. It's just that there's no space or need for it on the island. It's like saying you're not allowed to have a second brain installed in your skull. Allowing isn't part of it; there's simply no room in there for anything more, given its flawless design.

We don't mean to brag, but oh, are we happy! We know how wanting can feel like acid in the system when you don't have what you desire. Although that, too, can be turned into motivation! That acid can be upcycled into commitment to yourself: Don and I committed, and look at us now!

No, ha ha, no need to look at us for real. We haven't had a peel or fill in months, other than the DIY ones I snuck into my bags. Look instead at those petals meandering down through a blue afternoon, the bark strip-teasing from arbutus trees, the chalk pastel colours of the houses. Isn't it all just to die for? Don't you feel like you're already in heaven?

IIIIIIIIIIIIIIIIIIIIIIIIIIIII

One good burger, that's all I want these days. There's supposed to be a decent pub in the one little town on this island, but I have not found it to be decent. Have these people never been inside a real pub? This one is all glass and light and positive vibrations, which echo only too well the glossy menu of options—options that should never see print. White bean and chia burgers? Beer made with hemp? Gimme a non-organic break.

Holly and I diverge on a few minor points about this program/life-in-heaven thing we're trying out here. I agreed that smoking would have to go, and I said okay to a hybrid suv, but I never said beef was out. I will accept the backyard cows here gladly, if I can ever find one between two buns.

Instead I am driving her to a café on the other side of the island just to buy coconut sugar—whatever *that* is—because it's supposed to keep your brain healthy. When did Sudoku stop being enough?

||||||||||||||||||||||||||||||

Don and I started with a fresh slate when we arrived nearly nine months ago. No one knows what we did to get here; that's one of the main tenets of Can'Carma'Clear™. The past is over; the future is sparkly and clean. It's not that we're ashamed of what our past life looked like; we don't want to give people the wrong impression. It's not like we killed anyone ourselves! Everyone needs clothing, right? Everyone's got a choice about where they shop. We just provided a unique experience for them. We responded to a need.

Our business was called Babes & Babies. We convinced mothers that their babies' brains would be smarter if they dressed in matching outfits. When a baby recognizes their parent, they, unsurprisingly, have lower anxiety levels. That's what making strange is, after all: a baby looks at someone who has blonde hair when their mother has black, and instantly freaks out. *That's not my mama!* is what their cries really mean. We just wanted to strengthen the child-parent bond. Yes, perhaps the styles were a bit risqué, although I still don't see the issue with a young girl showing off her belly. What's wrong with a sweet little torso?

It was never *ever* our intention to encourage anorexia in kids under ten—although that's what the media will have you believe. We just imported everything from a country where people are much thinner, and their size six did not work for our six-year-olds. Oh, we tried really hard to get our seamstresses to follow our orders via quite a few emails, but unfortunately, they never seemed to respond. And that was well before the unfortunate events of last April, when fire consumed one of our biggest and most efficient factories. Polyester really does ignite with a passion.

In any case, that's all far, far behind us, and we've given ample compensation to the families. What the articles said, though, was that we turned the profits into roses, that we "washed that past right offa that cash" by coming here, to C*C*C*™'s answer to karmic debt. We found all of that rather crass, and don't even get me started on the cruelty surfacing in the online comments. Still, we paid up, and here we are, in our Western Canadian island paradise.

You might think that Don and I would naturally have children, given our business choice, but we have decided against them. We've seen how kids operate, witnessed adults reduced to tears over how cute their little girls look in their gold lamé sleepers, and watched their hearts growing larger right in front of us. Thus, we have decided—even though our own hearts jump at the idea of being parents, even though we'll never truly know what it's like to be a family of more than two unless we do it, even though we ache to watch a child of ours learn to walk, talk, ride a bicycle, deliver a speech, win a race—not to go there. We have equanimity. We have bliss. Plus, we have read the statistics on how each child increases the strain on the world's resources. And although we're both learning to relegate to a deep, deep place our desires about many things, such as hot fudge sundaes and plastic bags, this is the biggest desire we wrestle with.

Desire is no longer a part of our world. We have reached the other side of desire. We are serene. We are, well, we're *living the dream.*

IIIIIIIIIIIIIIIIIIIIIIIIIIIIII

Holly is getting seriously bored. She's been making lists of things to do that include *wash face* and *wear new shoes.* She knew she might be a little under-stimulated here, but she didn't want to listen to my suggestions of one of C*C*C*™'s places in New York City or San Fran. No, she wanted to get out of the country, to come up here into the clean Canadian air and *meld* with the scenery. Well, here we are. Melding has begun. My hair's so bushy, I feel like an unclipped hedge. Amber Rose Finch, our stylist-slash-angel reader, can't fit me in until next week.

I make my own lists, but they're a little more involved. Mostly they have to do with the house and the portfolios I've held onto, secretly. I've got an elaborate system of coding for all of them. Holly thinks I'm worrying over screwnail sizes, and that's okay. It's better if she has less to fret about. The whole debacle with the fires was harder on her than she'll admit, although I don't know how she can deny it every time she looks in the mirror. The knife-in-custard wrinkle between her eyes just won't go away, no matter how many good vibrations she channels its way.

IIIIIIIIIIIIIIIIIIIIIIIIIIIIII

We say "our" island, but it's just because we love it so. This island is home to hundreds of beautiful people (and a few that don't *quite* make that category—or, what I mean to say is that we just haven't been able to see that beauty quite yet) and an ecosystem that's nearly pre-contact in its wholeness. We coexist with this land's first beings, and let me tell you, they make better neighbours than the boomboxers and muscle-car collectors in the city. Some people complain about their gardens being levelled by deer and rabbits, but we smile and breathe deeply from behind our fences. We are safe and sound, and everything is in harmonious balance.

|||||||||||||||||||||||||||||||

God, these twisty roads are making my gut hurt. I'm tired and cranky and not a little bit pissed off at Holly for making me come, but while she natters on, I can't do anything but smile and nod like a fucking Chinese mechanical cat as I drive us home. After all, she'd remind me if I should complain, what else do I have to do?

Then, from out of nowhere, a giant deer steps onto the road.

"Holy shit," I yell. "Hold on!"

I don't have time to brake, and if I swerve, we'll end up in the ocean.

We both start screaming as we near the beast, but somehow, we don't hit it. We look back, still screaming, to see what's happened: we've just driven *under* a deer. She's got her front legs on one side of the road, her hind legs on the other, and she's eating from the trees.

I pull the car over. Holly and I look at each other; our mouths are useless gaping holes.

Slowly, we get out of the car to take a better look. It's a mule deer, a doe, at least eight times the size it should be. When it swings its gaze our way, we both run back to the car, get in, and lock the doors.

"This is just a nightmare," Holly says, in a robotic voice, her eyes closed. "I'm sleeping, and none of this is real."

I want to believe her, but I know we're awake. "No, honey. Open your eyes."

I squeeze her shoulder. When that doesn't work, I pinch her upper arm.

"It's not a dream."

Holly winces, opens her eyes, and looks back at the deer. It's turned away from us. We watch as it deposits a giant pile of shit on the road. It sounds like a pile of books being dropped.

"It's impossible," Holly whispers.

Before I can stop myself, my recent training kicks in.

"Nothing is impossible." Then, because I think I'm allowed to be a little pragmatic here, I add, "We only wish it were."

"Do you think . . . do you think it's real?" Holly asks.

There are a lot of things I could say. Like, *what do you think this is,* Jurassic Park? Like, *no, it's Rudolph gone all* GMO. But I must maintain my best self, or I will pay a hundred times over.

"Yes," I say. "It's as real as you and me."

But who am I kidding? This animal is realer than we'll ever be.

|||||||||||||||||||||||||||||||||

We're striving for enlightenment, Don and me. When you do this, you must deal with visits from thoughts that you don't want. We have thoughts that we recognize as being regulars, aside from the "this place is freaking awesome" ones, etc. There is the list of fears, including disasters: earthquake, tsunami, oil spill, meteor. There are the prayers: Dear God/Goddess, please don't let us get fat, ever. Please keep us both faithful. Please let us keep our money and live in complete comfort.

We are not proud of these repeating cries for help. But we are learning to allow them their time and, once that's done, to let them go inside pink thought balloons (thank you, C*C*C*™).

One thought that has never ever made an appearance in our brains, though, is this: if the animals on this island grow, then we will suffer. I mean, ha! What a crazy thought.

But they have grown. We are suffering.

It's been two days since we drove under that deer. We know now that it's happened everywhere—all the animals on this island are gigantic. We are trying to maintain our equanimity, but in the face of this, we are struggling. We know we are still blessed to live here and lucky to be in the program, but we're having a bit of a time with it all.

Are *blessed* and *lucky* what we're feeling now, with these animals at large, no pun intended? They're not just fleshy beyond their skeletons, or a little paunchy from too many Whiskas or Milk-Bones, not just pudgy around the middle from sitting on the couch's back watching for birds; it's not just a matter of stretched hides. These animals have expanded. Every cell has done it: bone, blood, hair, and hoof—a photographic enlargement, like a magician has said *presto* and pointed his wand at all the fauna, and *voila*, here they are, larger than life but very much alive. Big freaky creatures we think we know because they look just like they used to, except for one thing. They're huge.

The animals are fighting in the road and in the forests, no longer just minor scuffles between leashed dogs or territorial Siamese but real warfare, clashes of fur and fang that hurt our ears. More than that, it hurts our hearts.

Oh, truly, it's horrible.

We moved here—the obvious scouring of sins aside—to escape. Now, beyond the ambient sounds of amplified meows, barks, squeaks, and moans, we can hear no ferry whistles. No helicopters or sea planes. No one's leaving. No one's on their way.

Paradise isn't supposed to feel like prison! At least not the paradise I've been working toward.

We're, well, we're fucking trapped.

||||||||||||||||||||||||||||||

There was nothing in the literature about this. It has to be a joke, or just a special effects team here blowing off steam, getting their ya-yas out, probably as bored silly as we are. Can˚Carma˚Clear™ had only focused on the easy, natural beauty of this island, after all. It never mentioned the ennui, the mind-numbing effect of identical tree after tree, the cold ocean's grind against the rocky beach, its chaste white edge ruffling rocks so round and useless we can barely walk on them without sinking in up to our ankles. You can't even skip a stone here! And swimming? Forget about it. If you don a wetsuit for the frigid water, you look just like a seal, and the spectacular resident orca pod will mash you into dinner before you can gurgle for help. Oh, and that assistance the C˚C˚C˚™ promised, to get us comfortable, to address any glitches? Nope. Nothing. Once we were here and paid our fees, it just started feeling like real life.

Which is exactly what they promised, I guess. A new start, complete with all the idiocies of normal living—drunk mail carriers and leaf blowers and unstable wifi.

But *this*? This was definitely not in the contract.

It's bedlam.

It's been two nights since we came home to chaos. Once we were in our compound, with the gates shut behind us, Holly started to sob.

"The pool!" she cried. "Don, the pool!"

There was a Canada goose in there—except it was the size of one of those ride-on swans at theme parks.

Chicken-sized starlings were finishing off the cherries, squabbling over the last few jewels. Hummingbirds were as big as crows, hovering around the feeder Holly bought me for Father's Day.

(It's true, I'm not a father, but she still wants to celebrate the day because, otherwise, she asks, what else does a man have? I can't even own a pet because of her allergies. And she can't make us a baby, or so it seems, even though we've had the tests, tried for years, and have the moolah. She may have told you we're not interested in having a family, but that's just her sadness talking.)

God, though, I'm thankful we don't have a baby now. Imagine a housecat carrying her off in its mouth, dashing off beneath the rhodos to its secret lair, never to bring her back. God, that would be sick.

There's nothing worse than . . . We say this all the time without thinking, fill in the blank with whatever bad thing is at hand: soggy cake, burnt toast, wet feet, impotence, but it's not true. I know I'm not supposed to dwell on the negative anymore but screw that. There are always worse things. We're living in an Orwellian farm/zoo/garden/nightmare-come-true.

Right now, there's a rabbit lolling about in the actual garden, bloating himself on the biodynamic peas. Cats are scratching at the door with their three-inch claws. Holly's in the bathroom, submerged in a bubble bath, blasting Hawaiian chants for conjuring good things at full volume, trying to mask the insanity just outside our door.

In other words, farting in the wind.

IIIIIIIIIIIIIIIIIIIIIIIIIIIIIIII

We mustn't dwell on the negative. We know that every thought has power, and if we give a bad one its airtime, it'll only get stronger.

But we are getting worn down. Don and I are snapping at each other like the people we used to be after a long week of retail management hell. The grounds are decimated. The siding is coming loose. This morning we witnessed a murder—a massive cat ripped a cat-sized rat apart, right in front of the window of the room where we take our breakfast. We want to place a call and have a helicopter come take us far, far away from this hell, but they've placed us under martial law. Quarantine. If we leave, we become criminals.

Must get back to smiling. Must fake it till we make it. Must bury heads under pillows and repeat affirmations until everything goes back to better.

My affirmations: Get us out of here. Take us to Tuscany. Get us out of here. Dear God, take us anywhere but here.

IIIIIIIIIIIIIIIIIIIIIIIIIIIII

It's Day Three, and we wake up to "Thriller."

I groan and slap the snooze. I want to sleep, to stay in bed, in oblivion, but all of that is gone now. Skin-to-skin with Holly is still comforting, but the stench of warming feces from the yard will soon enter the house. I've got to get up and start the day by scraping the piles of poo away from the windows. Besides, Holly isn't in bed with me; she's been sleeping in the basement because its smaller windows don't let in the din quite as much.

The authorities don't want us to leave the house at all, let alone the island. They're worried about species-jumping. No shit. We're all worried about that. But we have been protecting ourselves with thought shields. We have been grounding ourselves in the moment, and so far, we're good. To be safe, I wear my wetsuit and motorcycle helmet when I go out, my version of a hazmat suit. I glove up, put my hip-waders on, and wear a paint mask over my face. Someone's got to maintain the property.

When I get to the back of our yard, I can hear a woman crying. We usually have little contact with our neighbours, since no one seems to do much living at their property line, but it seems someone's out here now.

"Linda?" I call, quietly, through the laurel hedge.

The crying quiets down.

I pull back a few branches to see her on the grass beside Cedric, her old basset hound. He's expanded to the size of a horse, only with much shorter legs, and he's lying on his side, not moving.

"Is everything okay?" I ask.

Linda looks at me like I'm crazy. Of course, nothing is okay. It's just a question. Automatic. Or is she reacting to my outfit?

"He's stopped eating, Don. He can't even walk anymore, with all that belly weight."

I've only ever seen Linda and her husband in perfect form, dressed in yoga gear and matching health sandals, pushing their pollution-free lawn mower over their acre of grass. Today she's in pajamas, hair flat on one side, mascara on her cheeks.

Then I realize that she's out in the open, unprotected from whatever might be in the air. "Shouldn't you be inside?"

"I can't leave him."

"Can I do anything to help?"

She shakes her head, eyes downcast. "What can anyone do? This—this plague, or whatever it is, is going to get us all."

Some people have started calling it that, a plague, as if it's been sent from the Bible to punish. For what, I want to know. Haven't we all been good people? Haven't we been living the good life—the C*C*C*™ high-fidelity version of it—in a place known for its gentle, loving politics?

"You could come for coffee," I say. "Holly made muffins last night."

She looks at me like I've suggested she kill her dog right on the spot. "I told you, I can't leave him."

"I'll bring you some, then. We could have a little tea party in your backroom, so we could keep watch . . . " There is no way Holly will eat out here in the air. This much dander alone could kill her.

Linda shrugs. "I guess so. I don't think I've eaten in days."

"Where's Larry?"

"Visiting his folks in Seattle." She looks like she's going to burst into tears again.

Lucky bastard.

I mean, poor Linda. She might never see him again.

IIIIIIIIIIIIIIIIIIIIIIIIIIII

When we're preparing our delivery tray for poor Linda, we hear about the killings. According to the CBC, the healers are beginning to hunt the big game. One bear's gallbladder is worth a fortune now. The few homeless that live here in their tie-dyed overalls are making bows and arrows, taking rabbits and deer down, roasting them on fires in the park outside the town hall. There are dogs on the loose, roaming in packs, looking for fights and getting them.

We mustn't think about it. Our feelings can enter whatever we cook, and do we want our neighbour to be crying all afternoon, even sadder than she is, because we stirred sorrow into her latte? Although she has admitted to a rather unsavoury past, we are keeping our hearts open for her. We are Americans, generous with our love. And our raspberry-ginger muffins too!

Before Linda came here, she was CEO of Clairol. In other words, she headed a world of chemical beauty enhancements, a company built on making women first feel bad about themselves and then, just slightly better, after buying into their propaganda and, therefore, their products. What she's really doing here on this island is the same as us, hiding out from the people who aren't happy with her methods of business, her quite questionable ethics.

Don and I just sold clothing, which, unless you're a member of a hot-climate tribe, is something you need for survival. We consider clothing to be an essential service. We provided a solution to a problem. Really, we shouldn't be here at all.

ıııııııııııııııııııııııııııı

Linda's cleaned herself up by the time Holly and I arrive in our protective gear. We assemble in her all-glass dining room. Outside, we can see Cedric, lying on the ground like he's already dead. When we all express our sadness at the state of affairs, we start the usual small talk.

"So," Holly says, although she knows the deal. "What brought you here?"

"Oh," Linda says. "The weather. The beauty."

We all look outside at the air, thick with feathers, dust, and dander, at the denuded world we live in. Can this really be courtesy of C*C*C*™?

"Same as us," I say. "Weren't we smart?"

I'm losing my touch. Neither woman laughs.

Holly's still getting nightmares about the biz. She was chanting *flame retardant, flame retardant* in her sleep last week, over and over. We'd just read a story about umbilical cords and how they have traces of over 130 chemicals in them now. Flame retardants were on the list.

Did she forget that we were saving lives, having that sprayed onto the wee pajamas we sold? There were no conclusive studies on any diseases actually being caused, but many cases of people *not* being set on fire. Not to mention all those parents with complete peace of mind!

I'm getting all worked up here. I've got too much time on my hands now, as my small kingdom becomes a wasteland. My only job, aside from maintaining my stocks, is to shovel the shit away. And apparently, to console the neighbours with my shoulder to cry on. The scent Linda's wearing reminds me of some gay old times in Paris, pre-Holly.

I pull my attention back to Cedric.

"He's lived a good long life," I say, trying to get her to look at the colossal beast.

Linda starts sobbing against me. Silk washes, right? Holly's shoving a napkin in Linda's face, but she won't take it.

"It's okay," I murmur. "I've got more shirts."

||||||||||||||||||||||||||

After a few minutes with Linda, I start to sneeze and get headachey. It must be all the products left over from her reign; surely, she has a lifetime supply in her five-car garage. We only kept one small box of our products—just in case we ever knew a child they might suit.

Right now, there's a squirrel outside that seems to be about a size five. Maybe we should dress him in neon fuchsia leggings and a crop top, just for old times' sake.

Linda has been consoled with carbohydrates and caffeine and my husband. Cedric is not long for this world, but what can we do? There are battles worth fighting, and there are battles worth walking away from; once Linda starts really losing it over her "baby," I put on my protective gear and run back home.

That isn't no baby out there, honey. That there is a dead old dog.

||||||||||||||||||||||||||

Evil.

It's a word I used to love. Before all of this, before the cleanse and the move, I used to use it whenever I could. For example, the weather is often evil, raining for weeks, Holly's baking is evil if it's too rich, she's evil when she wears her red stockings and garters.

Wore, I mean. Past tense. The past has claimed that particular activity.

It's Day Five, and what I think about more than anything else is how small we are. What we used to dominate, we don't anymore. Last night there was a mouse in the kitchen, and it took Holly and me an hour to trap it in a cardboard box. Fortunately, the innate nature of each animal hasn't changed: a mouse still likes peanut butter and cheese. The squirrels are still climbing trees, although the branch breakage is comical. The raccoons sleep all day, rub against the house as they try to get comfortable in their new under-the-deck accommodation.

But just like knowing there is always something worse, there is always something to be thankful for. Now I am thankful that there are no primates on this island, other than us. Shit, monkeys would be awful. Evil, I mean, and not in a good way.

⁕⁕⁕⁕⁕⁕⁕⁕⁕⁕⁕⁕⁕⁕⁕⁕⁕⁕⁕⁕⁕⁕⁕⁕⁕

We are running out of food. One of us can survive on pasta and peanut butter but not the other, and that other is getting grumpy. Oh, I know the teachings: grumpiness is better than anger, which is better than hatred or depression, and we should always be reaching higher on the list of emotions to get to the least harmful one, but I can't get above grumpy. My beautiful garden is destroyed! The thing I loved most in the world, to wander for hours while smelling my flowers—especially at dusk, when the blues got bluer and the jasmine and the nicotiana smelled more wondrous—is no longer possible. So, yes, I'm grumpy.

And goddammit, there's a dead dog at the back fence and the deer keep crapping on the lawn furniture. Yes, Cedric is gone from this world. How long he'll remain resting against our hedges like a flipped-over cement truck is anyone's guess. I've got more important things to dwell upon.

Other than lamenting my lack of quinoa and fresh arugula, I'm spending all my time hatching a plan to leave. We do not want to be criminals, but we can't stay here like this. I've heard of some sort of night kayaking service that's started up, and a swimmer who made it to the mainland, and even a kite surfer who kept on sailing south. It seems it will have to be by water that we leave this prison.

When I am nearly asleep in a mid-afternoon semi-silence, the most phenomenal idea drifts in: we can escape in a Flintstones-type boat made out of a hollow log, something we can lay in and kick our way across the strait to the USA.

Forget the nap. My mind's suddenly busy making plans. Tomorrow, we'll head to the beach and find the ideal specimen.

Except I can't leave the house. Shit! Fuck! This is stupid!

But then, I hear it. A voice, coming in from the cosmos, telling me that there must be a way. How else have we made everything else come true?

I engage in a serious debate with this voice for a few minutes until I'm slapped back into truth.

We're trapped, but we're okay. We're still breathing. We have so much to be thankful for. Something will come to us. It always has.

Sleep, come sweetly, please. I will chemically assist you and think only about rescue. Even as the giant cats howl and the rodents chew on my tulip bulbs and the last blades of lawn, I force myself to repeat a new affirmation: help must be on its way.

But if I should die before I wake, that wouldn't be so terrible today.

||||||||||||||||||||||||||||||

On Day Seven, I wake to a silence so deep it feels like I'm still sleeping. Even Holly, asleep beside me, seems to barely be breathing. I run to the windows and twist open the blinds.

It's happened. They're dead. All the animals are flat-out where they took their last breaths. There are so many, it's like they all came out of hiding to die in the open air. Oh, it's horrendous wreckage—fur and turds and twisted bodies everywhere.

I just stand there, staring into the backyard, counting the animals. Five raccoons, three cats, two dogs, a bunch of rodents, a whack of sparrows, seven deer, and a bald eagle the size of a glider. This yard used to be filled with birds—normal-sized, alive. Once I even saw a peregrine falcon in the pear tree, a small rabbit in its grasp. Last year, right after we moved in, that one tree gave us five hundred pounds of fruit. Now it's empty, other than that one giant pear near the fence.

Wait a second. Out there, amid the carnage, the decimation, there's still a beautiful pear? How the hell did the animals miss it? How did we miss it? It won't be pear season for months.

My mouth begins to water. I have to have it. I have to taste it. I should wake Holly, but no.

I'll bring it to her in bed.

I *will*.

Quickly, I get into my faux hazmat suit. The animals don't pose a threat of attack any longer, but who knows what's growing on those carcasses? I don't even want to imagine the size of the maggots that will come.

It feels like I'm going out trick-or-treating: the scary landscape, the get-up, the sweet prize at the end of it. Sweetness!

I step around the dead animals in the yard and make my way toward the tree. The air smells like wet dog and old pillows and BBQ smoke, alongside the usual crappish odour—some people have begun cremation, it seems. Thank God for the boots. The destroyed lawn is slick with excrement.

Once I get within a metre of the pear tree, my old salivary glands really start pumping out the juice. I can practically taste that glorious fruit!

Then, on a high branch, I see something else. Not the pear.

A nest made of rags and bones.

Out of it, poking above the ragged edge, there's a head.

It's the smallest living thing I've seen in days, and it's looking at me with clear, blue eyes.

It's a baby. Good God. A human baby. Saying something in babble, to me.

||||||||||||||||||||||||||||||||

It's worked.

My God, it's worked.

The Law of Attraction has truly outdone all of its other efforts today. It had to circumvent our outward resolve of not wanting children, of becoming fine with that, being turned down by various adoption agencies because of our media history, and my little white lies about saving the planet and our equanimity. It had to deke around our reasoning to get to the raw hunger inside of both of us.

We really *do* want to be parents and couldn't imagine life with only the two of us, forever and ever in this big, perfect nest of a house. Although the timing's a little off, Universe, we thank you. Thank you!

Also, a shout-out to C*C*C*™, in case this is also a part of our package!

We're calling her Apple, even though she was found in a pear tree, because of her sweet rosy little face. A little irony—or a Bible reference—never hurt anyone. Thank you, Jesus!

When Don climbed up on that ladder in his wetsuit, helmet, and hip waders to get her this morning, I just fell in love with him even more than the day we met at the swim-up bar, when he asked me if I wanted a massage. Here was a man who had to work at tenderness, who still ate Twinkies in supposed secrecy, who punched a heavy bag for hours before he could even talk to me in the mornings, reaching out to remove our baby from that tree.

"Lift your visor," I called out. "She might be afraid if she can't see your face."

He did it, even though we still didn't know what might be in the air. I'd stopped caring at that point because, suddenly, there were more important things in life. I had a little girl to take care of! Damn the flight attendant mantra of putting your oxygen mask on first before assisting your child—when it comes down to it, something in the blood just kicks in, and you have no problem sacrificing yourself for the good of your babies.

Because I'd watched so much birthing footage over the past few years, I just did what came naturally: I took off my shirt. When Don passed her down to me, we were skin-to-skin at first contact. I didn't even care that she was covered in filth, and peeing, as he handed her over.

She's my baby. I made this happen.

All we needed, after all, was just a little faith.

〰〰〰〰〰〰〰〰〰〰〰〰

Apple is a beautiful child.

We're watching her sleep in the centre of our bed while we discuss our plans to escape. Holly's got this hollow log idea, which just might work. It's only a few kilometres to the next island, where there are animals of normal size, trees with leaves, lawns still grassed over. I've heard of wolves swimming to islands. Why not us, in a magical boat?

"Isn't she peaceful?" Holly asks.

"Sleeping like a baby," I say.

I give Holly a hug, smell her aromatherapy shampoo, feel her breasts against my bare chest, before she starts to scream.

"Oh my God! Don!" She's pointing down at her own feet. Suddenly, they're Ronald McDonald feet. Two feet long. Then her legs start.

Before I can say a thing, it begins to happen to me. My skin begins to tingle and burn. My bones creak, my joints pop, and my muscles start to bulge.

Holly shrieks, grabs Apple, and runs outside, smashing her own head on the doorframe as she goes.

My head is at ceiling height. I crouch down just before my torso expands, get onto my belly and crawl out of the room, squeezing through the door as if I'm being born.

I find my family on the front deck, my wife naked like me—clothing doesn't grow, apparently—and my baby in a sweet little sleeper covered in purple sequins.

The baby has not grown. Apple is as small as, well, an apple, in Holly's branch-sized arms. She's bawling.

"She must be scared," I say, and my voice booms out like an air horn, which only makes her cry harder.

From our new vantage point, we can see the whole neighbourhood. Decimation, dead animals, dirt, all the giant homes stuck in a wasteland. We used to have a view of broadleaf maples, western cedar, arbutus. Now we can see the ocean, the calmly rolling blue.

Then I remember the pear. It's still there! I lumber over to the tree, reach down and pick the fruit, which is no bigger than an almond in my gigantic fingers, and hand it over to Holly. Maybe Apple's hungry. I'm starving, but the crying baby comes first.

As we try to mash up a little fruit with our big mitts, over Apple's wailing, we hear someone yelling at us from the backyard. "Don! Holly!"

It's Linda, big, like us. Stark naked too. When I wave, it feels like I'm moving an umbrella through the air.

I look over as Linda tries to cover herself up with leafless branches. But that's not where my mind goes first; my enormous stomach roars louder than anything else. She's been home alone for days—surely, she's got extra food.

llllllllllllllllllllllllllll

Dear Any Kind of God, C*C*C*™ or otherwise: it's Holly here.

You know that I've always relied on lists as a tool for getting to the heart of desires. So, here is my list. (Please hear me!)

Please let us shrink back to our normal size again.

If this isn't possible, please let Apple grow big, to be just like us. She's going to be so sad to look at us and not see her kind.

Please don't let the Death come like it did to the creatures around us.

Please punish whoever brought this upon our island. We thought this island was filled with wonderful people with pure hearts, but there must be someone here who's got some wickedness or serious karma needing to get worked off. Sometimes I just want to be able to send those people off in a giant boat, a prison ship adrift in the Arctic Ocean. Please make this happen. If it's Linda, well, so be it. Who are we to get in the way of fate? And by the way, it just isn't fair to the rest of us who are really trying to be better people.

Please let there be a tailor in this mess of a community, preferably with European training.

llllllllllllllllllllllllllll

We may be naked, giant, hungry, and cold, but we're still alive. Still a family, with Linda on board, all of us big ones wrapped in bedsheets, just staring into Apple's sweet little face.

I can't fit into the house to check my stocks, let alone press tiny buttons on tiny machines, and I'm probably losing thousands.

The bigger worry is what else might be in store for us. From our vantage point, we can see other heads poking up in the neighbourhood. We can see what kind of situation we're dealing with, and who might be coming to call.

We've got to start cooking these chickens before anyone else gets their hands on them—maybe the squirrels too. Definitely before nightfall, when we'll have to figure out some kind of shelter.

C*C*C*™, you've really outdone yourself this time. Making dreams come true, aren't you, at just a little cost? Whether or not you created this expansion, I know that Apple was planted by you. Why would you do this? To test us, see what we really want? In the midst of chaos and uncertainty, our true natures win out, and you give us a child.

What I'm not sure of is whether the baby is meant as reward or punishment. Did we pass or fail?

||||||||||||||||||||||||||||||

I want to go home. I can see American soil—it's just one island over. To hell with the pioneering spirit, manifesting our destiny, our American birthright! Forget about clearing spiritual debt. All I want to do is calm this darned baby down and go home.

What did my mother do to make us stop crying? A little brandy on the soother, maybe. Ha! If I had any brandy left, it wouldn't be Apple drinking it.

Lullabies. She sang to us, although I'll be damned if I can remember any of them. Through my tears I start singing the first song I can think of.

"I'm bringing home my baby bumblebee. Won't my mama be so proud of me?"

It sounds like pure poetry. I just want to go home and see my mama in Ohio and introduce her to Apple. Having kids does that to you, makes you want to reconnect with those who've shunned you, those who swore they'd never say your name again.

But who am I kidding? She'd be scared as hell of me. Everything is different. I don't know what any of this means, or where home is, or if we'll ever get out of this mess.

Wait. Apple's stopped crying now! She's smiling at me! Oh, what am I whining about? I'm such a lucky duck. This is home, isn't it? Me and Don and this tiny little girl.

Oh say, can you see? She's small, but you can still see that beautiful smile. *The Lord is good to me . . .*

Johnny Appleseed, amen!

||||||||||||||||||||||||||||||||

Day One of Creation, Take Two.

Or is this Take Three we're on now? Even God gets a restart, I guess. But if C*C*C*™ is behind all of this, there are going to be some serious suits against them if any of us survive it.

And yet, Holly's singing. I should be more like her. See the good in all of this.

She's handing me Apple now, a baby transformed by a mother's love.

"Take her," she says, beaming.

There's a look in Holly's eye that I don't recognize. A purity to her gaze. Angelic, even.

"She's going to make all of this better."

I've heard this promise before, I know it. I've felt my heart lift with the possibility. I ask the baby, "Now where have I heard this before?" but of course, she doesn't know the answer.

But when I look into my miniature daughter's eyes, even from way up high, I can see something there—something I hadn't noticed before. A movement, from deep within them, like a shutter, as if her pupil has a mechanical centre, adjusting for light, as if all her being is focusing on her new-found daddy, recording this historic moment for evermore.

Today, a dark afternoon in February, on the way home from her job as a hotel housekeeper, Catherine goes into the 7-Eleven and buys her brother John's favourite candy: Junior Mints. She checks her hands for obvious grime before reaching into the box for five mints. That's the rule, five per serving. She isn't counting calories or points or carbs. Five at a time means she can leave the box alone for the rest of her walk home, which means she is free to watch for waxwings.

The waxwings always appear in February on the coast, when the berries of the holly trees glow red against the daily gloom. But Catherine hasn't seen one this year, and it's nearly March. She's always thought of March as *martyr*, when it's shortened to MAR., on account of Lent and the way she used to feel giving up the things she loved. She never understood how it worked: if you offered your suffering up to Jesus, did it really make Him happy? As she walks along, she can hear the Junior Mints jumping in their box, safe in her purse. God doesn't get her candy anymore. But she still believes in some things the Bible talks about, like the Golden Rule and miracles.

Because of this, Catherine looks in open windows—mostly at dusk—in case John's inside one of the houses she passes. She rescued a stray dog once, brought him into her suite where he sat on the couch, staring out the window, while she called animal control. Five minutes later, a man on a bicycle spotted the dog from the road and came knocking. It turned out that the spaniel lived three houses down; Catherine had thought he was lost when he'd only been on a little walkabout. Still, the man was happy to have him back. He still says hello to her when they pass on the sidewalk.

Maybe John, her missing brother, has lost his memory, or has just gone out for a wander. Maybe he's in a kitchen nearby, washing dishes, and she will see him from the street.

Catherine knows she is well-loved at work even though people might think she's a bit naïve. She carries her water in a glass honey jar and wears suede boots in the winter. She buys lottery tickets, picking numbers based on ages she's loved most, years she had the best times of her life, which leaves out, naturally, thirteen and twenty-one, as well as all the numbers beyond twenty-six, because she isn't there yet. At thirteen, she had terrible acne and the largest breasts of anyone in school, and even friends she'd known since preschool stopped hanging out with her. She spent that whole year helping the librarian at lunch and the kinder- garten teacher after school; she was particularly good at cutting out hearts, freehand, no fold down the middle to ruin them. And snowflakes, too, and letters that look like balloons.

At twenty-one, she lost John, the person who had loved her despite, and because of, and anyway . . . He used to play around with her name, calling her Cattail and Catkin, Catapult or Catbird, and it was as if he gave off oxygen, like a tree, because any time she spent near him made her feel more alive. With no parents left, except the kind they visited in the cemetery, now and then, they'd been alone together against the world.

The police gave up on the search for him years ago. John went missing when he was her age, twenty-six, and now he would be thirty-one, and every day, she sends her thoughts out to him with a coating of light attached so he can see them and follow their beacon home.

Where are the waxwings this year? The hummingbirds are plentiful, making the air buzz, and robins with their cocky attitude, and sparrows everywhere. All of the regular birds are abundant and, therefore, boring. She wants exotic, rare; she is a speciesist when it comes to birds.

Once, when she'd needed it, she'd lived in a hospital at the edge of the Fraser Estuary, and the only birds that had caught her attention were the visitors, the fancy accidentals that should not have been there. A whooper swan. A Steller's sea eagle. An American avocet. A prothonotary warbler. Oh yeah, she's all about the bling, she thinks, which is a laugh. Her boots are leaking, her umbrella sags on one side, and her scarfless neck is cold and bare. Fancy, indeed.

||||||||||||||||||||||||||||||

The search continues into March and April, a daily ritual for Catherine despite the warming temperatures and the abundance of so many other lovely birds. She needs that waxwing, its crest an elegant variation to so many round, predictable heads, because sighting it would mean that her brother is fine. That's what she's told herself every year: the waxwing is a soldier, back from war, and John is lost in action, in another kind of war altogether.

Oh, the hero's welcome she'll give him, the celebrity he'll become!

Once a week, as she has for all these years, Catherine walks past the bus station to check for John. She saw him there once, before he disappeared, on a day when he hadn't known she was following him, and she'd watched as he did his thing. His thing was a secret, she knew that much, and she was no snitch! Still, when he looked up from talking to a blonde woman in ripped pants, after giving her a small packet and taking rolled-up cash, his face had turned red beneath a blank and empty stare when he caught her watching.

As usual, he's never at the station.

||||||||||||||||||||||||||||||

In October, Catherine begins a new kind of search. She's been dreaming of black things, gigantic crows and umbrellas and bruises. She has not seen a waxwing all year.

Catatonic. Catastrophic. Cataclysmic.

She begins an exhaustive search, obituaries from when he first disappeared, or as far as Google will take her. *John Bryan*, she types. *Dead. Death of John Bryan, suddenly.* And *Young man dies tragically.* She reads of young men dying tragically all over the place, even one with the same name as her John, who met his end by driving off the ferry dock. But the photos are not of her brother. The details are all wrong. The drugs are new ones—some hidden in other drugs, so that you don't even know you're taking them until it's all over, just like that! They say it's a peaceful way to go, but that's no consolation.

She turns to searching for his description next, in case he isn't dead, only at large. In case he might be wanted by someone else. She enters: *Small-eared man. Afraid of rats. Double-crowned. Voice sweet, like cinnamon.* Nothing comes up.

Then, after dinner, there's a face at the patio door. A fluffy orange cat wants in, and after Catherine opens the door, he lets her pick him up. She can feel him purring. He's got a name tag, unlike the dog she rescued, and while she calls the phone number on the tag, Dexter, the cat, gets a can of tuna.

The woman on the other end of the line is ecstatic. Her baby has been missing for twenty-four hours. When she arrives a few minutes later, she lifts Dexter from Catherine's arms, and it feels like he doesn't want to leave her. Catherine begins to cry. The woman throws twenty bucks on the coffee table for her effort and makes a quick exit.

Caterwauling. Catapult. Catalyst.

After they leave, Catherine makes a sign on poster board to fit into the front window. *Welcome Home, John!* it says in bubbly letters, coloured like the rainbow. She stands on the lawn to admire it, to make sure it can be read from the sidewalk, and then she strings up white Christmas lights around the window frame, just to give it more punch.

A few days pass, and the sign begins to buckle; a few more, and the letters fade. Neighbours start to look away when she meets them on the sidewalk, once they've asked about the homecoming. Still the sign remains in the window. Still the lights shine, attracting moths and dust.

Catherine begins to leave open cans of tuna on the porch, and Junior Mints, and bowls of bright red berries she gathers from the park on her walks home, just in case. She sits on the front steps at dusk and sings songs about coming home and a hymn she's heard at the church around the corner about putting your burden down. *Come to me*, it says. *All who are weary.*

John was tired all the time before he disappeared. She knew that could mean low iron, but didn't that apply mostly to women? It could have been her; she remembers her mother saying that she was exhausting, on more than one occasion. But that was back when she ran the circuit, making a race track of the path from living room to hallway to kitchen to dining room, round and round. That was back when she had to sit on her hands to keep from picking at the wallpaper or the label on the HP sauce or whatever scab was ready.

She's tired now too—tired of waiting, and the waiting makes her tired.

At work one afternoon, Catherine crawls into one of the beds she's just made. She takes off her uniform and slides between the cool sheets and frees her long hair from its plastic clip. She turns to the window and sees her brother's face in the clouds above the park. She closes her eyes.

When she opens her eyes a while later—did she fall asleep?—there's a man, right in front of her, in a uniform.

"Catherine," he says. "Are you okay?"

"John!" she cries and leaps out of bed to embrace him. "You're really here!"

The man looks toward the door. "Better come," he calls, and her co-worker Shirley bustles in.

"Ryan from engineering's going to get you home, Cat," Shirley says. "He'll take care of you."

Catherine is still hugging him, unable to let him go. "I am home," she says. "In my brother's arms. Shirley, this is John."

Then she is in his arms, fully, because he's picked her up like a bride; they move from the hotel room down the hall, into the elevator, and out through the staff doors to a blue Jeep, where she's set gently down in the back seat.

"No air bags in the front?" she asks. "That's why I'm back here?"

"Sure," Ryan says. "Safe and sound."

They drive the short way to her apartment—without her even needing to give directions. Of course, he knows where she lives!

"Where have you been?" Catherine asks, calmly. She doesn't want to upset him or scare him away.

He's pulling up outside of her home. "Let's get you inside," he says. "Then we can talk."

He wants to tell her! And look, he's smiling at the sign in her window, even though it's barely legible anymore, giving her a thumbs up.

When they're inside, she gives him another hug. "I can't believe you're here!" She holds him at arms' length. "Promise me you'll stay?"

"I'm here," he says. "I'm not going anywhere."

Barbara and Jack sat at the kitchen table, scrolling and eating loud cereal, a level of comfort between them that made it acceptable to belch, softly, without fear of judgement, as long as an *excuse me* followed. Both of them weary from end-of-semester stress and studying, they still had the energy to scan the news headlines on their phones, to take turns reading out bits of tragedy or outrage.

The biggest story trending that December morning was the anniversary of the École Polytechnique shooting in Montreal, when fourteen women died at the hands of a lunatic.

"Horrific," Barbara said, and rubbed her face, as if to wake herself from a bad dream. "You never know, do you, when a madman might strike." Then, in the next breath, she said, "I'd like to feed the birds again."

It was dizzying, this feat, the leap from despair to hope, something Jack had a hard time navigating. Had she forgotten that she was leaving him in a matter of days for sunny California and wouldn't see the birds finish the seeds they put out? And what about the shootings since Montreal?

"Sure," Jack said. "I miss the little guys."

Barbara had moved in with him about nine months ago, over spring reading break, and the seeds had moved in too, but he'd had to shut the operation down after a squirrel came into the apartment through the balcony door and lived with them for three days until, finally, it went into the live trap he'd bought.

Today she wore her bunny blouse: it was off-white, semi-sheer, like the shed skin of a corn snake, and on it, stamped like leaf prints on a sidewalk, were rabbits. Jack knew she knew that he loved it, and she wore it more often than she used to. He wondered if he should wear T-shirts imprinted with leave and berries, cotyledons and lichen. He was an animal man, and she a plant woman, in simple terms, but he was wearing a T-shirt that featured Pluto, the planet demoted and then partially redeemed. And he wore it not for her but for underdogs everywhere, a gesture of solidarity. It also glowed in the dark, which made both of them giggle more than it should when they lay in the drafty bedroom, making love with half their clothing still on. They did not get out enough.

Jack wanted to leave the cereal and phones and thoughts of madmen on the table and go back to bed, where he would slither in next to her and resume their body press, their retreat, and attempt to stop time from advancing. But there were scarves to be wrapped around necks, coats and gloves to don; there were groups of smart and good people waiting for them to help them study for their exams; there were exams, and then, much later, there were those very same necks to unwrap before falling against each other in the closest pub, where, despite it being exactly what Jack wanted to prevent, they would toast to another day having passed.

||||||||||||||||||||||||||||||

After breakfast, they headed for campus, but not before they passed Russell, the man who slept beneath their window, two floors down on the street. He was still asleep, in blankets Jack recognized. He'd tried to help Russell with quilts, pillows, food, music, attention, and these things had worked to placate him, temporarily. Some days he was lucid, and he and Barbara could talk to him, just like they talked to one another. But recently, when the weather turned from bad to worse, things had started to change. Russell was getting as bitter as the wind.

He didn't seem to recognize them anymore, and in the early morning hours for the past few weeks, they'd been awakened by his screams. Thankfully now, he didn't stir.

A block from school, a young guy who Jack called "the poet" joined them; he wasn't a student, but he liked to hang around academics, a natty notebook in whatever pocket was handy.

He'd eavesdropped on them at the laundromat a few months ago, when Barbara had been deeply in love with a particular type of begonia, growing "like static flames" on their balcony. The poet had liked that phrase, and said so, which prompted her to pull out her phone like a proud grandma and brag with photos. Since that day, the poet, named Joshua—an infantile name for a poet—had hung out with them.

"Because of your focus," he'd said, when they'd asked him why. "And your lack of shame about being slightly freaky, in a good way. Plus, you're able to have normal conversations," he continued. "You just choose otherwise when possible."

Neither Jack nor Barbara could argue with that, so he'd stuck around ever since.

The three of them parted ways at the university; Barbara to her people, Jack to his, Joshua to wherever he went, with plans to meet for lunch at the cafeteria.

Barbara and Jack were not a fancy couple, nor one that made plans together beyond lunch or passing their exams, but he loved her with a certainty that caught in his voice like a swallowed bone. After exams, she was planning to put herself on a plane and head south, to where the land bloomed anew in January. Succulents, ice plants especially, were her passion, and in Hamilton, Ontario, they only bloomed in the floral sections of the grocery stores.

And this was right, this was appropriate. She studied plants with more attention and reverence than any nun ever read the Bible—sometimes Jack could feel her eyes on his head, trying to classify the lank curls that grew there.

At semester's end, it was anyone's guess as to her heart's next move, but at least for a semester or two, she would be gone. Jack's heart was crumbling, disintegrating deep inside; and although he was an animal man, well-schooled in cardiac anatomy, if he jumped up and down, he swore he could hear the bits and pieces making music, something slowcore, mournful, and spare.

IIIIIIIIIIIIIIIIIIIIIIIIIIIIIIII

That night, after a lot of studying and a little tired loving, they woke to screaming, a panic flooding their systems like twenty shots of espresso.

"It's okay," Jack said to Barbara. "I'll deal with it."

It was the last thing he wanted to deal with. He wanted to ignore the suffering just beyond the window and turn toward her delicious warmth and go back to sleep.

"Thank you," Barbara mumbled, before sliding into what he imagined were dreams made of satin and spider webs, gauze and coloured shadows.

It was okay to turn to each other instead of to the pain beyond the window, Jack reasoned, because they had tried before to help, and nothing had come of it.

Russell, most likely, was not being attacked by a pit bull, not a victim of a hit a run. His leg was not broken, his fingers still hung from his hands. Visibly you could not spot one thing wrong, unless you looked into his eyes.

Then you would feel it, the helplessness: his, the world's, in the face of a brain gone sideways.

Jack lay in bed with Barbara against him, breathing softly once more, a moth drawn to his heat and light. Russell had quieted down.

Jack's father had been a drunk, a chain-smoker, and a gambler, and he'd been front and centre for it—a car ride with a drunk dad behind the wheel was the perfect gamble, after all. "Let's see if we can make it home both alive and without a cop noticing" was the game of choice. Sometimes Jack thought the smoke that filled the car was what saved him, despite the fact that it had given him asthma. That smoke was cellular, like endoplasm, holding the family together, at least until his father finally ran off for good.

His family seemed unbelievable to Barbara, if she got him talking.

"How you survived it is a miracle," she said.

But Jack knew there were worse situations; he'd had food and shelter, after all, and although he hadn't needed to scramble into ditches for beer bottles, he'd done it anyway, on the long walk home from school, for candy money. That his father had forbade his mother from getting her driver's license, or that he'd disappear for days at a time with the one car, leaving them stuck on bikes or their own two feet—*Good enough for Jesus*, his father used to say if they complained—these were the things Barbara got upset over.

The truth was, those spells when his father was gone were the best times: nights of uninterrupted sleep, mornings of peace and quiet. He hadn't felt like he was living a cliché, a parody of the alcoholic's family life, not until she pointed it out. It was their normal, and both he and his brother knew other kids with way shittier lives than them.

Their man on the street was like a *New Yorker* cartoon on irony, haunting Jack's sleep more effectively than his father or memories of childhood. But he didn't need to revisit all that stuff, did he? Did the animals in his care rehash every moment they'd felt stress? He was one of the ethical ones, not those madmen spraying soap in the eyes of rabbits to see if it hurt them. The payoff, if he used animals, had to be worth the price, over all else. If he could find a cure for MS by manipulating the myelin sheath of a mouse, was that not worth the process? He was getting closer every day.

Jack credited his father, in fact, for making him the person he was today. Not because he'd taken his example and done the opposite, although that was exactly what he'd done. Not because of genetics, either—nowhere in the family tree was a branch sturdy enough to hold him and his future Nobel Prize. No, it was all because of the night his father had shoved him into a hole in the frozen lake.

He'd been depressed, obviously. It was as clear as anything now. But kids weren't allowed to be depressed back then, not unless something really big and really awful had happened. Plus no one in his family would even consider seeing a "headshrinker," so even if they'd recognized it, his therapy would have been the advice to suck it up and get his shit together.

Jack could remember only vague bits of the year that preceded the big event; one year of high school over, he'd been fine, managing, the quiet nerdy kid in Grade 10 who kept to himself because it was easier that way. He'd carried a couple of friends over from elementary school, and they ate together, rode the bus together, and gamed together when he was able to use his brother's laptop, which wasn't often. Then his brother just up and dropped out of Grade 12, right before Thanksgiving, and took off with a guy heading to Mexico, to surf the winter out. Jack felt stranded; he *was* stranded. He started spending all his time in his room, in a kind of stupor.

"You stoned?" his father asked him. "High on some weird shit?"

Jack just stared into nothing. He felt like he was inside a television. Everything seemed to be outside of himself, beyond the glass, people trying to reach in and touch him.

After a couple of months of this, and a couple of beatings, after missing weeks of school, his father and some buddies took steps to fix the problem. Under the light of a clouded-over moon, they nabbed Jack from his stinking bedroom cocoon and carried him to someone's pickup truck; then after a short drive, they carried him from the truck and onto the frozen lake, littered with ice-fishing huts. Jack was too out of it to even protest. They stood him upright, unwrapped the blanket that swaddled him, and then they dropped him through an enlarged ice-fishing hole, directly into the frozen lake.

All Jack remembered was that it felt like a blister popping, that kind of painful relief. The opposite of a fairy-tale kiss to wake him up, it worked the same magic, that frigid water. He emerged, aware and alert, angry and ready to get back to it. He had no explanation to give his father, nor did he thank him. But he'd finally done something right as a parent. After the guys helped to warm Jack up, his father handed him a flask of rye. The sweet burn of it in his throat, the clarity it brought, made it all too clear he could drink like his father—and that he might be better off avoiding the stuff. But he was fully, completely awake.

And Jack was awake now, listening to Barbara breathing. He wanted to help Russell, but he couldn't. If only the brain could be fixed like a bone. If the spirit could burn once more, a match to the wick. If the heart could yearn for things beyond medication that only ended up killing instead. Jack wanted to help more than Russell: those poor souls trampled on the way to pray in Mecca a few months back, children without clean water, mothers unable to cope with their sick kids, polar bears stranded on small carpets of floating ice, the world that burned and maimed and raged. He wanted to fight back, but there was no way he could take on any of it.

Now, insult to injury, he could hear sleet hitting the balcony. Russell cried out again, and Jack pulled Barbara closer until it felt like they were nearly one. She was pliant in sleep, and he wanted this particular moment to never, ever come to a close. Well, he wanted the sleet and the crying to stop, but not their merged bones, their heat, even their sour breath.

They were, in his dozy state, a sculpture in a field, a Barbara Hepworth or a Henry Moore or maybe more like a Giacometti: a made object in a natural setting. Rain or shine, they would stay rooted on the spot, though sheep may graze at their knees, though birds may alight on their ears, though sleet may needle its way through their surfaces, storm by storm.

Insult to injury? The weather had no agenda, except for the agenda people attached to it. Same with that hole in the ice, not made for a person to be pushed into but simply for entrance of hook, line, sinker, and bait—and for the potential exit of the fooled fish, a thrash of silver and fight—although the hole he'd been pushed into must've been made a lot bigger, for him. No way he'd been that skinny as a kid.

Just before Jack philosophized himself to sleep, a thought barged in. More of a slogan, really, something popular these days to support small businesses. *Keep it local.*

What would happen if Russell got pushed like he had, into frigid water? What could come of a plunge like that? A stripping away—a return to original state, baptism and all of that? Would he slip away quickly, or fight for ascension, kick toward the lantern light, dully glowing above?

Jack was filled with such longing that all chance of sleep was gone. He was going to wait out the morning with his love in his arms, and then, once their exams were over, he would put this idea to poet and woman, to see if they would help him lower Russell into Lake Ontario.

Barbara's lips were as dry as the husk of an old runner bean as she slept on beside him. The crazy ideas continued. Maybe he could ask her to marry him, to accompany him to the grave with love as their limo. Whatever would stop the line from "Four Strong Winds" from playing on repeat in his aching head. "Still I wish you'd change your mind . . ."

"Will you marry me?" he mouthed into her ear, quiet as a breeze. Then, from below, Russell cried out again, and this time, Barbara woke up. But Jack didn't ask her anything aloud; he put his own chapped lips to hers and said good morning, and they groaned their way out of bed to go write their exams. Another day closer to the end.

IIIIIIIIIIIIIIIIIIIIIIIIIIIIII

Two days later, exams done, the three of them met at Oasis, the restaurant they reserved for celebrations, although none of them looked up for a party. Still, Barbara ordered the tenderloin, thick coins beneath a mushroom cream sauce; the poet got his usual deconstructed burger, everything on the side; and Jack splurged on a salmon filet presented where it had been cooked, on a cedar plank. Plants and animals, fusion again.

Before the food arrived, Joshua spread some photographs on the table. He liked to snap pictures of random moments and show them later, asking them to guess where and when.

In one photo, Jack's own neck shocked him, taken from the back. It was too slender, barely there at all, and his shoulders! The bones made gables at their outermost edges, as if his shirt had been hung on sharp hooks. Barbara sat beside him, her hair's waves catching the light in regular intervals of beauty, while Jack seemed to have a heavy head, unable to hold it completely straight. With a neck like that, no wonder.

It was attention the poet had caught; they'd been at a lecture on the intersection of biology and art.

Still, the picture made Jack wonder if he was capable of doing what he was about to suggest. None of them were athletes, but altogether, he hoped, they'd add up to one.

After two quick pints, he had to grab onto a chair to steady himself when he got up to use the bathroom.

"Are you woozy?" Barbara asked, and laughed approvingly. It was a game between them, to get the other drunk, despite Jack's father's history, and they weren't any good at it.

"I'm okay," Jack told her. "Just tired."

With finals over, the break of nothingness between semesters loomed. Plus he'd botched at least one essay on his philosophy final (oh, the existential worry of it, too much awareness of his awareness), and Christmas was only days away, like an earthquake that was not only predicted but confirmed, and then the tsunami of her leaving would strike.

When Jack returned to the table, he launched into it—his idea to help Russell. To his astonishment and delight, they agreed immediately, wide grins all around. He couldn't tell if they were humouring him or really on board, but he kept his hopes up.

"We'll need a rope, around his waist or something," the poet said. "We have no idea whether or not he can swim."

"What about a life jacket?" Barbara asked.

"I have a rope," Jack said. "No jacket."

Over more drinks, they came up with the plan. Well, not so much a plan as a manifesto. They would save Russell. Come hell or high water, they'd grab him, nab him, then get him down to the river!

They just had a few logistics to work out.

> Problem #1: None of them had a vehicle.
> Solution: Taxi.
>
> Problem #2: The fight in Russell. They'd seen him throw punches as well as fits, sometimes both at once.
> Solution: Something strong, offered to him in the guise of a warm beverage. Hot chocolate laced with NyQuil?

Problem #3: Immunity to such innocent drugs.
Solution: Triple the dose?

Problem #4: Not alerting the cabbie to the crime.
Solution: Acting like it was normal. Plus, luck?

Problem #5: Killing the guy instead of helping him.
Solution: The rope?

|||||||||||||||||||||||||||||||||

They went back to the apartment to enjoy another few beverages, keep planning, and wait until nightfall. When the poet drank, he became goofy, effusive, obstreperous. When Barbara drank, which was news to Jack, she laughed and laughed and went weak, as if it went right to her bones and muscles. Jack tended toward verbal diarrhea and the munchies. He slowed down on the booze once the peanuts came out. Those recent memories about his father were a little too fresh.

Jack's grandmother's solution for everything was always food. No surprise—she was a classic grandma. Sad? Cupcakes. Can't sleep? Peanut butter toast and a banana. Constipated? Prune juice smoothie. Lonely? Apple pie. Chest cold? Soup—chicken or mulligatawny, mustard and onions plastered on the chest. Really, really hungry? Mashed potatoes and cups of gravy, lots of meat.

He believed they could lure Russell in with something so delectable that he could not refuse. Cherry Delight, for some reason, was all that came to mind—another classic that Jack's Grammie used to whip up monthly. Graham crust, Dream Whip, and cream cheese middle, a can of cherry pie filling spread on top. Perfection. But how would he get this into Russell's hands? It was all goop and crumb.

Barbara came up with a better solution and set about creating it: warm cookies. It might appeal to the long-hidden kid in him, and as long as it wasn't a major trigger, then it would work. Who could resist melted—*melting*—chocolate chips? Apparently not a trio of drunks—it was a wonder they saved any for Russell at all. But they reserved a few and tucked them into a yogurt tub for transport.

ⅢⅢⅢⅢⅢⅢⅢⅢⅢⅢⅢⅢⅢ

Even in the frigid air they could smell Russell from ten feet away. He was rolled up in a tortilla of dirty sleeping bag and orange afghan, shaking and muttering to himself quietly, until they began talking to him. He emerged, rabid and lunging.

"We're on a missive!" Joshua declared, and although Jack detected the boo-boo as soon as he said it, no one corrected him. Was he still that inebriated?

"Have a cookie!" Barbara cried. "They're amaze-balls."

Language skills were going to the dogs, but no one cared— they were on a mission and nothing, not blood alcohol levels nor punches nor sanity would stop them.

"How 'bout it?" Barbara continued. "Warm, still. I made them myself!"

"Here," Joshua said, and presented the hot chocolate-NyQuil cocktail. "You can keep the cup too, bro."

Russell had stopped thrashing about with as much intensity and was beginning to focus on each of them, one to the next, then back again.

He took the cup and drank sloppily, greedily. Perfectly. Then he set into the cookies. His grunts of pleasure were symphonic—or at least like hymns—to Jack's ears.

Russell drank and ate. They stood and watched, stomping their feet to keep warm.

When he'd finished his cookies, he turned away from them, about to retreat into his nest. Jack recognized his pillow as the one he'd left for him a year before—its white Snoopy pillowcase gone brown. They had to stop him before he softened into a drugged sleep, but Barbara and Joshua were busy singing a jubilant version of "Away in a Manger," arm in arm. One passerby threw change at them, either thinking they were carollers or just to shut them up.

"Russell," Jack called. "We're going to a party. Wanna come? Are you game?"

He swung his head slowly in Jack's direction, his eyes turning to vacant once more.

"Fuck off," he slurred. "Tired."

They had to act quickly.

Once Jack got their attention, Barbara and the poet stopped singing, and while he made certain Russell stayed put, they managed to flag down a cab almost instantly.

"Here we go!" Jack said. "Russell?"

"No!" he said, over and over. He was weaving now, rubbing his beard and his head, kicking at cardboard and nothing. "No! Fuck off! I'm no trouble. I'm no trouble."

"Let's do it," Jack said, and together, the three of them grabbed him and hauled him into the taxi's back seat.

"A little too much holiday cheer," Barbara told the cabbie, who seemed blasé about it all. Somehow, they all ended up in the back seat with Russell, pressed around him like big packing peanuts, trying not to breathe.

"To the docks," Barbara said, and luckily, their chilled-out driver didn't say a thing.

||||||||||||||||||||||||||||||

None of them ever looked at the forecast in Hamilton because nothing the weather threw at them seemed to make much difference in how they lived their young lives. They had the down jackets, the Gore-Tex, the toques. They had their (non) polar opposites. Youth wasn't supposed to be spent mired in the details of precipitation. But if there was one day on which they would have been wise to check the predictions, it was this particular day. There was a storm on deck—a humdinger, a bazinger, a big, honking thing about to bury the whole bottom of the province within hours.

Russell had fallen asleep against Jack's shoulder. The poet flourished a rope and a blue tarp from his satchel like they were magician's supplies. What the tarp was for was anyone's guess, but Joshua had insisted on bringing it when he spotted it in the front hall closet. Barbara was still singing carols, this time along to the radio. And with Russell's filthy head resting on his shoulder, his mouth and nose taking breaths of such slight depth, Jack felt close to passing out.

When the snow amped up its productivity, the cab slowed sensibly, but they inched toward the lake nonetheless. Jack knew he was supposed to announce an exact destination, but he had no idea where to pick. All they needed was seclusion, a dock, and easy access, but the whole area looked like it would do the trick, aside from the lights that burned dimly through the chunky snowfall.

Yet, no. Slowly Jack's brain had been coming back to alert mode, and suddenly, he knew with sober clarity that the idea was a lemon. But then the poet nudged him, signalled that this was the spot, and so he asked the cabbie to stop.

"Here?" he said. "You sure?"

"Thank you," Barbara sang, like a jingle. "This is it!"

She and the poet unfolded themselves from the car and stood outside, completely stunned by the snow, tongues out to catch the giant flakes.

The driver looked back at Jack as he tried to pry Russell's fingers from where they'd wrapped around the door handle. Even in his stupor he was somehow still fierce, guarded, rigid.

"He okay?" the cabbie asked.

"Oh, yeah, he's just . . . " Jack's brain struggled to grab an explanation that didn't involve them having drugged this guy before being about to throw him in the water. "He's just having a diabetic episode," Jack said. "His father works nearby, and he has the—he has what he needs."

"No shit? Is he high or low?" The cabbie popped open his glovebox and pulled out a bright orange tube.

"I'm not sure, but—"

"Doesn't really matter for now," the driver said. "If this works, he's low and we've saved him. My brother's diabetic, so I keep this on hand. Here, open up his mouth a bit more. This needs to make contact with the gums."

And just like that, he reached over the front seat and squirted some kind of goo into Russell's chocolate-smeared mouth.

Russell's eyes popped open and he jerked his head forward and hit Jack right in the chin. "What the fuck? What the fuck?"

"Whoa," the cabbie said. "That was pretty fast."

"Help, over here!" Jack called to the two snow worshippers, his eyes watering, teeth and jaw aching from the blow. Together they managed to get Russell out of the cab and pay the driver, who was pleased as punch to have saved somebody's life.

Once the cab drove away, all they could hear was the whisper of the snow collecting above their prisoner's murmurings. The air smelled like creosote, and snow, and then piss: Russell had peed his pants where he sat in the snow, leaning against Jack's leg. But other than the odd strain against the rope they tied around Russell's wrists, once the cabbie was out of sight, he was strangely still.

"Are we sure about this?" Jack asked. "I mean, maybe this whole little outing has been enough for him today. He seems pretty mellow."

The poet laughed. "He's just taken a piss against your leg, my friend. If that isn't cause for a little swim, then I don't know what is."

Plan, still on.

But what if Russell didn't want to wake up? Had *he* wanted to, that night his father pushed him under? He hadn't wanted anything; he was numb. And when he came out? Not numb. Grateful? Hardly. Angry? Angry. And certainly more alert.

He'd seen Russell angry. That was not going to be pretty, if they were successful.

What had happened, really, that night he went under the ice? If he looked at it as a scientist, there were two possibilities. One, that the plunge had been an example of an acute stressor, causing a normal, healthy response in his body—adaptive stress that had made the blood flow to the areas it was most needed. Fight or flight instead of rest and digest.

Chronic stress was the villain; Jack had been reading papers on that since high school and had been witness to it, too, in his own mother. It didn't take a psychiatrist to recognize that she'd been under tremendous strain with his father around, and once he left for good, the changes that began to happen. She would never turn her grey hair blonde again, except from a bottle, but at least the light had come back into her eyes.

Acute stress, something sudden, short-lived, immediate, and then gone—that was the thing mammals were good at handling. Survival depended on it. Pain here, then gone, dealt with, over.

The second possibility was that Jack's plunge into that lake had been an ancient hydrotherapy cure. A cold immersion bath. And hadn't he read about cold exposure being as effective for depression and anxiety as drugs or electroshock treatment? Jack would have dismissed it all as more alternative mumbo jumbo, in the camp of homeopathy, if he hadn't been the case study. He was the proof.

So, sure, he could pretend that they were doing the right thing here. Doctor Jack, prescribing, administering a medication. But he wasn't a doctor. Who really knew what was wrong with Russell? Or what might change with a plunge?

It was all just a drunken caper, and now they had a captive man tied with rope who'd pissed his pants in possibly the biggest snowstorm of the decade, down at the docks with no way back home except walking. Cold water shock could just as easily set in if they ever got Russell into the lake; he was no teenager, lethargic but otherwise healthy—he was unwell, unstable, and now, unconscious. But what other choice did they have?

Jack untied Russell, then lay him down completely on his back and pillowed his head with the coiled rope. Barbara and the poet were busy making an army of snow angels until Jack stopped them at three apiece.

"Get up off your butts and help me," Jack said to them. Why were they so mesmerized by this damned storm?

They laughed like maniacs when they looked at him, stern-armed, with his beard and toque gone completely white.

"Come on," he pleaded. "We have to get serious. This is a bad thing here. We're in deep shit."

Just then, Russell began to moan.

All their cell phones were either dead or elsewhere, and the snow was continuing to make its wet descent—and then Jack had it, somehow. Another idea. A better one. The way out of this.

The idea cut a slash through the surface and it held. This snow was perfect! They would build an igloo and keep Russell safe, like Snow White in her glass coffin, until someone better came along to save him.

He knew that, in the morning, life would return to this corner of the city the way the songbirds and forest animals had surrounded Snow White's resting place. The mobile canteen would bring hot coffee and donuts, sandwiches and hotdogs for the dockworkers. Then, from somewhere in the back of his slowly clearing mind, another way out came to him: the Mission to Seafarers.

Once upon a time, his Uncle Ed had volunteered with them, on a Christian crusade to help the needy, and they had a chapter here in Hamilton, probably within a block or two of where they stood.

His uncle had told Jack stories about the men who'd been out at sea on merchant vessels, how they'd come to him desperate for a decent place to eat and to treat medical emergencies like jock itch and lice—some of them had been away from home for years. After a prayer or two, he'd helped them out as best as he could, directing these seafarers to the closest mall or hospital before their ships left Lake Ontario, bound for open sea once more. If they could do that for complete strangers, surely they would help a local man, even if he hadn't come by sea.

Jack told Joshua and Barbara the idea, and either the booze was wearing off or they were bored, because they both agreed it was brilliant. How had he ended up with two people so amenable to his wacky plans?

"Let's get to work," he said, and got them rolling the heavy snow into balls.

"I thought igloos were made from cubes," the poet said.

"We're working with fresh snow," Jack said. "We can't afford to be shapist."

They worked, unsteadily. Slowly. But soon enough, something was taking shape.

Joshua cried, "We have done a glorious deed!" once the walls around Russell were complete. All of them were soaked, and panting, with cheeks as red as baboon butts.

"Wait," Jack said. "We're not done yet."

He unfolded the blue tarp they'd brought and together they laid it over the top of the snow walls, then secured it with more snowballs as best as they could; snow on plastic was not a match made in heaven. Still, once they were finished, they stood back from the creation and felt a glow burning from within, and it wasn't from the exertion alone. Or that was how Jack felt, at least. Maybe a Christian glow—a pre-rescue glow.

"He won't be missed," Barbara said.

Jack turned to her, aghast. "Wow," he said. "That's quite the statement."

"No, I mean now, with the blue roof. I was worried he might get plowed under in the night." She swatted his arm. "As if I'd say a thing like that."

They stood in the snow, falling less intensely now, and Jack reached for her hand. "Of course not," he said. "Thank you."

She squeezed his fingers and they stopped talking, listening to the light sizzle of flakes hitting the tarp.

The moment was broken by the poet's watch alarm beeping.

"Time to—get up?" Jack asked.

"I'm on a routine," Joshua said. "I wake myself up in the early morning to catch dreams for poems."

"Oh boy," Barbara said. "We'd better get you to bed then."

"No, no," he said. "This is golden. Gold. Or at least straw to be spun." He began turning around in circles, chanting *Rumpelstiltskin*.

"Let's go," Jack said. "Russell's sleeping."

"And that means we can sleep too," Barbara said, yawning and wrapping her arms around Jack.

Their apartment would be quiet, their dreams uninterrupted, their gathered warmth sustainable for hours and hours. But then, Barbara would leave him.

They should stay with Russell, shouldn't they? Make sure he was okay. And what was wrong with a little more snow fun? It was okay to enjoy it, Jack realized, like Barbara and Joshua had. Why was he always so hung up on doing something? Could he not just take a damn moment and simply notice what was around him? Appreciate it all? Just live?

That was where the trouble lay—Barbara had helped him to live in the moment, and that had gotten him nowhere but here, about to lose her. About to be alone again. And just like light could trick a person, mirages and reflections, shadows and blinding beams, his "keep busy" program had fooled him. It had worked, oh yeah—after his plunge, Jack had done a one-eighty, pushed his way through classes he'd been failing, rose slowly to the top, stayed out of his father's way, tried not to think of his brother and how he missed him, focusing instead on his own kind of escape.

Russell was just another project, another thing to fix and check off his list.

Barbara needed to go, and he couldn't stop her. Her area of expertise was found nowhere near Hamilton, Ontario, where the land—fertile and once able to feed the province—was nearly all buried beneath concrete and asphalt.

But maybe, if he made himself as desirable as possible, she might migrate north again, when conditions permitted. Or he could visit her in the sun, if invited. Maybe he'd even look up his brother, who'd been sending cryptic postcards for years, waves and palm trees on them, with no return address.

"Let's make a snowman first!" Jack cried. "To watch over Russell." This was perfect snowman snow, and no time to waste it.

David and I were still awake at three AM. The moon wasn't full, that wasn't the reason, but the Perseids were doing their August trick, showering meteors like streaks of sleep dust from the sandman, mocking us.

I reached over and belted myself in with David's arm, even though it was hot in our room. I needed the comforting.

Until yesterday, when I'd taken her to a small lake outside of town, our daughter, Anna, hadn't worn summer clothes once. I thought it was about breasts, one growing faster than the other, or maybe because of her belly, but from what I could tell, Anna had become more proportionate as she'd grown taller.

I hadn't been all that worried: she hadn't stopped eating or gone berserk with exercise the way my friend's daughter had the year before; she wasn't sneaking out, getting older guys to boot liquor for parties. Until yesterday, I'd just put it down to fashion.

Beneath the safety strap of my husband's arm, I cried. I was at a complete and utter loss.

Then he said, "Shhhh. Listen."

An owl hooted, just outside the window. It hooted again, sending its quiet plea into the darkness.

"Cool," he said. *Cool*, at a time like this? "We should go find it."

But it was cool. Our city street was lined with trees, but no owls had come a-calling before.

"We'll never find it," I said.

Then I heard Anna's bed creak. I removed David's arm and sat up.

"She's heard it too," I said. "Let's go."

||||||||||||||||||||||||||||||||

Yesterday—a hundred years ago—we'd been the only swimmers at the lake.

"Now will you take your layers off?" I begged Anna, from the water. "No one can see you here."

To my surprise, Anna stepped out of her jeans and pulled off her hoody. There she stood, my pale, beautiful girl in a black bikini, hugging herself as if she'd never been hugged before.

"Come in!" I cried. "It's nearly bath water."

Anna walked to the edge and yelped when the water hit her feet, but she didn't run. Instead, she took a few steps and dove right in. When she surfaced, she was both a new person and my long-hidden daughter, dark hair smoothed against her skull, generous smile bigger than it'd been in weeks.

"Happy now?" she asked me. Smiling still.

Was I happy! We swam for twenty minutes, alone in that small lake, floating and laughing like we'd always done before daring to climb onto the private raft at the other side.

It was when Anna lifted herself onto the floating dock that I saw them: her inner arms, laddered with cuts—no, scars—at least twenty per limb. Whiter than her white skin, they seemed mostly healed. But I knew what they were—had been schooled on this latest trend, never thinking I'd have to face it. Still, I asked all the same. "What happened to your arms?"

"Oh, I keep scraping them on my dresser drawers," Anna said. Then, with a face as pink as lemonade, she flopped onto her belly and changed the subject to her job-search troubles.

There had been more than scrapes or lines. There were hashtags. Asterisks. Little stars to mark the spaces.

IIIIIIIIIIIIIIIIIIIIIIIIIIIII

Searching for an owl in the darkness seemed better than lying there sleepless, making a list of dangerous items around the house. Would we have to go through the babyproofing again, only locks instead of elastics on the cupboards? Knives were obvious, but what about forks? The can opener, the sharp edge of the old peeler?

Already I'd mentally locked away anything that might turn into a weapon. Boxcutters, scissors, staples. Nail clippers, frameless mirrors, even Q-tips: maybe they were as dangerous as those commercials showed, that sharp stick beneath the soft tip, hidden until damage was done.

What had I missed? What signs had I filed under "normal teenaged behaviour"? That day when Anna wanted to wear high heels to school and I'd said no. Or the day Anna flipped out because there was no cereal in the house—had she begun it then? Or maybe it was the day the boy she liked said he only wanted to be friends. Or during her first period, two months ago, or after failing the math test? What about us forbidding her from bringing home the girl who'd punched her mother in the face?

Where had I failed?

Because he was into anthropology, David tried to get me to see it another way when I started crying yesterday, once Anna was out of sight.

"Maybe it's the new rite of passage," he'd said. "The modern way to mark this time of insanity." When that didn't make me feel better, he continued. "Scarification was huge in certain cultures. And I don't think she has a death wish."

I'd jumped when he said that. "But what if she cuts too deep?" I asked. "What if it's a step?"

His only answer had come as a thick embrace. It wasn't much comfort—our daughter was the one who needed arms around her. If only I could wrap Anna in a sling again, wear her all day long, put her to sleep between us the way I had for her first two years. Despite so many warnings about over-coddling, that had never been a mistake.

‖‖‖‖‖‖‖‖‖‖‖‖‖‖‖‖‖‖‖‖‖‖‖‖‖

Now Anna's door was opening. She, too, had been summoned.

"Did you hear?" Anna whispered, from our doorway.

"Yes," I whispered back. "Let's go find it."

What the bird would tell us was anyone's guess, but we needed to get closer, to confirm that it wasn't all in our heads or just a ringtone we were hearing.

An owl ringtone. *Who, who who who?*

The three of us descended to the front door and walked out into the night. Clouds had rolled in, blocking out any chance of seeing meteor showers. The owl called again. It was such a deliberate cry—no chatter or gossipy nature to it, no demanding plea. The owl had no competition in the night sky; there was a confidence in its calls.

It was just like my grandfather, delivering the readings at Mass when I was a child. No matter how odd the story—water to wine, hands into Jesus's gaping wounds—or how impossible the instructions, any doubters became instant believers when he read. His voice demanded good posture, a clear head, a pure heart. This. Is the Word. Of the Lord. The amen that followed was nearly evangelical in enthusiasm, nearly tipping over into sacrilege for the subdued Catholic Church.

Yet despite this early exposure, I'd given Anna nothing to believe in—beyond herself and a mostly beautiful world beyond the door. At Anna's age, I'd gone to a Catholic school, knew good from bad, heaven from hell, how to sing a hundred hymns. When I'd recited the prayer before Communion—*Lord, I am not worthy to receive you, but only say the word and I shall be healed*—it had felt like renewal, like another chance at getting it right.

But the Church didn't always make a person this warm and fuzzy. Maybe Anna's cutting was as Catholic as you could get: self-flagellation. Maybe the anorexics were the modern-day dervishes, shunning the body and the pleasures of the flesh for some bigger plan. If that were true, then bulimia was religious too. Sinning, punishment, forgiveness at the toilet-as-confessional.

It was too late to give Anna a taste of ceremony or a new look at religion; David and I had both gone AWOL on church before we'd even met. Was it unfair of us to keep this away from Anna? Had she missed out?

The owl called again. David cocked his head, pointed to the tamarack tree at the edge of the front lawn. We shuffled over to stand beneath it, and it hooted once more.

"Mom," Anna said. "Doesn't it scare off its food, making all that noise?"

I didn't know the first thing about owls. My hand itched to find the mouse, to Google it. But I'd been on the computer all day, looking up case histories of cutters, clogging the search engine with questions to cover up the ones I could not ask: *What is so bad about this life we've given you? Where did we go wrong?*

"Maybe it isn't hunting right now," I said. "Maybe it just needs to talk."

Each low hoot vibrated softly in my chest as the three of us stood there, listening. After a minute, we heard a distant reply. The owl—our owl—seemed to compress itself into a tight ball of brown and white feathers before launching into the air on its massive wings. Then all we saw was the shape of it vanishing into the cloudy night, closer to whatever stars might be falling beyond.

A question had been asked, and an answer had lifted itself out of the darkness.

The girl, Carolina, sat on the couch, knitting up a storm. The wool she'd been using for weeks was a deep, thunderous grey, so it seemed that she was knitting, and becoming, a landmass—a geological disaster waiting to happen. Evacuations would begin when the eruptions did, yet no one knew the data. No one could make any educated guesses about when this girl would blow.

Rules in a family were only obvious when you held that family up to a mirror. Jen should have made ground rules, but she wasn't a rule-maker. She simply lived a particular way, and her husband and son followed her lead. Now, here, as of three weeks ago, their mirror had shown up as Carolina, daughter of her husband, Ben. (Yes, Jen and Ben. It was a terrible joke).

Carolina was here with them in Vancouver because she was eighteen, finished high school, and got booted out of her mother's house in Regina at the beginning of the summer. She hadn't visited in seven years, through no fault of Ben's, and now she was here, in their condo, trying to figure out her next step. Jen and Ben and little Cody were a step. *Step*mother Jen had to repeat this to herself: just one little step, one plank in the staircase. It had better be a long staircase.

"We don't knit in this house." Jen had fantasized saying this for weeks now.

Oops, she just said it.

Carolina looked up, nodded once, kept clicking her needles. The woollen mass kept growing, and now covered her bare legs as far down as her knees. Of course she took Jen's statement as observation, not commandment.

Jen's blood was boiling. Because of the knitting, yes, but also from the infernal silence overpowering the noise of the needles, the weirdness and lassitude that exuded from the girl on her couch. That was Jen's couch! A private place, now inhabited by a squatter! In every waking, non-interacting moment—even in her sleep—the girl was a lump.

Maybe that was it, the root of her anger: Jen was afraid. Silence and laziness had long been the enemies, and she'd tried to befriend them, but she was a doer, and so was Ben, and Cody— well, a young boy never really stopped. Now these entities were here, mocking her, right in front of her face. If she were a reli- gious person, she might have been able to call upon the ideas of virtue and sin, but she wasn't, and any attempt at asking the only religious person she knew—Ben's mother, Kathy, who lived a few neighbourhoods away, near Queen Elizabeth Park—for guidance, had just left her simmering with frustration, for all Kathy offered was a benign smile and an offer to offer the suffering up to Jesus, a tit for tat kind of thing.

And Ben wasn't all that helpful, either.

"Well, at least she's knitting," he said. "That's something."

But making what, Jen wanted to know. Was that sludgy thing going to turn into something?

Jen had to create a plan of attack. Instead of relaxing on the balcony in the precious sunshine, perhaps she would make a list, go through each room, imagine scenarios that she would not tol- erate from Carolina, a sort of babyproofing like she'd done when Cody began to crawl.

Tambourines and shakers and a couple of sand blocks, left over from Kindermusik, lived in a basket beneath the bookshelf.

It was there that Jen's list began: no music before nine AM or after eleven at night. Of course, Carolina hadn't touched any of them.

"Do you play an instrument?" Jen asked, while she pretended to do a deep dusting of the room. "Or what about singing?"

Carolina shook her head, then actually said something. "My mother made me take ukulele."

"It's good for the brain," Jen said, although she hated the plinky, childish sound of the thing because it reminded her of a bad trip she'd taken to Maui with her first husband, who'd gotten so wasted he peed off their balcony and got them kicked out of the resort.

"No comment," Carolina said.

No comment? She'd said *no comment*? What the hell was that supposed to mean?

"Ha," Jen said, which meant nothing at all. A laugh lie. Total BS. She picked up her pace and dusted her escape out into the front hall.

IIIIIIIIIIIIIIIIIIIIIIIIIIIIIIIII

On good days, they were like one body, Jen, Cody, and Ben, a unified sum of parts. They just worked well together—limbs and brain talked to each other without saying a word. And Cody, his little plum cheeks pressed against Jen's legs, saying he wanted to marry her? Perfection.

All of that had been relegated to the past, once Carolina-of-the-couch arrived. You couldn't see Ben anywhere in her face, with its pallid slopes, its poked-in eyes. What salacious whispers had begun the journey from wooing Ruthie, his ex, to this replica of her?

Jen wanted to know that younger Ben, so she could do her own whispering in his ear: *Keep it in your pants, honey. Wait for the good wife.*

Oh, she was a horrible person. But self-admonishment didn't really count, did it, if you smiled while you said it?

What little she could get from Ben about the relationship did not satisfy her. Jen could just not make the differences between her and the ex add up. It didn't compute, that Ben could love her and have loved that woman too; how could he even call it by the same name? But maybe love was like hockey: the game encompassed slow, bumbling circles, and breakaways too, yet it was all still hockey. Ben was just getting a lot better at the game.

Except, with Carolina around, there was no breakaway possible. How do you play the game while piggybacking a sullen, indolent teenager?

Alongside the dream of a wonderful father-daughter bond—something that Ben had been denied despite years of trying to remain connected with Carolina and her mother, who seemed to have moved every year or two, following a trail of mediocre jobs in small towns and foul-weathered cities in the middle of Canada—there had been dreams of freedom; a built-in babysitter, everyone had enthused, when they'd heard the news of her arrival, as if she were a new appliance. Jen and Ben had allowed themselves to dream of long dinners over sumptuous platefuls of local, colourful food instead of Cody's beige palette, a whole bottle of wine disappearing between them.

That dream had promptly fallen apart: Cody and Carolina did not magically hit it off, and the one time Jen had dashed to the chiropractor, leaving the girl in charge, she'd come home to a crying boy, a bad-tempered girl, and a chocolate-milk-sodden T-shirt in the sink. *She yelled at me for spilling!* Cody had cried.

It was all Jen could do to not imagine Carolina's neck between her hands as she rinsed and squeezed the shirt out. But visualizations had power, and she wasn't ready to be responsible for anything so dark.

||||||||||||||||||||||||||||||||||

The next day, instead of broaching the subject with Ben—how would that conversation go except *your daughter is a vortex of negative energy, and I can't handle this anymore*—Jen decided to get serious. The girl needed guidance; she'd give it.

Mother to invention is necessity: she'd post her lists. She shuddered at the thought of a ratty notice taped to a cupboard door, another above the towel rack in the bathroom, but what else could she do? She'd laminate them, at the very least, use a welcoming font, avoid black ink—or would the prettiness undermine the message? No. It would have to be Arial Black. These rules would not be negotiable.

Kitchen: The blue bowl is off-limits to anyone but Jen.

The bowl was the first gift she'd been given—from an aunt— when she moved out on her own, at eighteen, and the fact that it remained unbroken was a sort of miracle. What else did Jen have from that twilight time between childhood and this grey zone of responsibility and gloom? Nothing.

Sesame seeds, crumbs, flakes, and grains are not dust. They are not to be swept onto the floor as if invisible.

and

The sink is for washing dishes and produce. Please use with frequency, drain the sludgy water after, and clean out the stopper basket. The sink is not a garbage can.

Occasionally Jen herself would slop her leftover cereal or apple core into the sink, but only because it was a cultural habit brought along from her family. She was going to break it for good, right here.

The list-making was meant to help, but it made Jen feel queasy. She wasn't *that* anal, was she? She'd always thought of herself as easy-going, and people called her chill, relaxed, laissez-faire. Mostly they said these things on the playground, or at parent-kid get-togethers, when she made it a point to remain calm on the outside even while she was raging within. Luckily, Cody was a good kid, and she'd never had to freak at him in public. Some days she worried he was a little *too* good; that he should get riled up more, protest, rebel against something.

Were these lists the gateway to a darker version of life? *This is your life now*, she told herself these days, which never failed to make her teary. She didn't want a dark life, goddammit. She wanted the old one back. The lists would continue. They were all she had.

Carolina came into the kitchen while Jen was writing out the next item.

> Juice is a once-a-day beverage, 8 ounces max.
> Water is our regular drink of choice.

The girl pulled the mango nectar from the fridge, poured herself a tumblerful, then tucked a box of chocolate-topped cookies under her arm and left the kitchen, leaving the juice bottle on the counter.

"Carolina," Jen called out. "The juice."

No response. Headphones or insolence? She was too tired to investigate.

For the first time ever, Jen regretted turning down Ben's offer to join him and Cody on their hike in Stanley Park to find pine cones for an art project, although he'd invited Carolina to go before he'd asked her.

And she could say nothing. Nothing at all.

Because here was the stumbling block, the clincher, the deal-breaker, if she were to ever suggest a deal, beyond the fact that Ben was desperate to make this father-daughter thing work: Ben and Cody shared no DNA. In every other way they were related—they *related*. Two peas in an edible pod; so cute together that Jen could just gobble them up. But she could not say anything about this girl in the house; she shared Ben's blood and Cody didn't. When they sat side-by-side on the couch, their hair was identical, as if it had come from the same can of squirrel-brown paint.

No, Jen was in no position to say one word. Instead the words grew teeth and began to chomp at her from within, gestating creatures that were all hers. If she didn't let them out, they might destroy something vital—everyone knew that was how diseases got started. So, who would hear her? Who would offer a sympathetic ear, advice, a partner in whatever crime might be necessary?

|||||||||||||||||||||||||||||||

The following morning, while Cody was in the bathtub, the phone rang a song of salvation. It was Adrienne, Jen's friend on Salt Spring Island. Jen could almost smell the sunlight on the salt-pocked deck railings, the briny front yard ocean, when Adrienne, in her beautiful salvation of a voice, asked, "Are you ready to shoot her yet?"

She knew. Even though she was childless, and had never been forced to share her space with anyone other than her mother-in-law, once a year, out from Toronto to impart urban wisdom and disdain, Adrienne knew what Jen was going through.

Don't cry don't cry don't cry, Jen told herself, but it was no use. The tears came anyway, as part of the package.

"Come visit," Adrienne suggested, in her cashew-latte voice. "We'll go see Julianna."

Julianna was an angel reader on the north end of the island. A woman who could see the future in a person by tuning into the beings she saw, or felt, around them. She was Icelandic—the J was a Y in the mouth, and it was all a part of the tradition, the tuning in. In Iceland, the fairies took precedence over roadway projects, as real as indigenous gravesites or wildlife habitat. Jen had visited Julianna with Adrienne once before, but only waited while she got her reading, there to escort Adrienne home in case the news was bad.

It was never bad, though, according to Julianna. She only tuned into the good things, or at least the parts that offered potential.

Jen needed potential. Were there angels hovering around her, like fruit flies? Sometimes she felt a sort of static halo; maybe Julianna could make it into something useable. Something that might make her stop placing hexes on a certain girl in the house.

As soon as she'd hung up on Adrienne with a promise to attempt a childcare feat of wonder to make the trip possible, a promise that made her heart feel winged, Carolina shuffled into the kitchen.

"My laundry stinks," she said, through sleep-gummed lips.

The fury that shot through Jen's blood was as efficient as radioactive dye; scanned, every inch of her would glow.

"Well," Jen said, pointing at the utility room, "the machine is just behind that door."

Carolina said nothing. She didn't even acknowledge that Jen had spoken; she just poured herself a giant mug of coffee, then squirted half a cup of chocolate syrup into it and added the same amount of cream before taking herself and her breakfast into the living room.

How could she do this? It was—

"Mom!" Cody called from the bathroom. "I'm done!"

Jen tried to shake her anger off like a bird shuffling its feathers and found Cody standing in the tub, shivering, a landscape of rich bubbles around his calves. The air was ripe with chemical roses.

"Where'd you get the bubble bath?" Jen asked, although she knew: it was Carolina's.

"I borrowed a little bit," he said. He pronounced it *borr-e owed*, something no one had tried to correct since it was so damned cute.

"Uh huh. Well, let's get you cleaned off." Jen sprayed him down with the showerhead, making him shriek because it tickled.

Once he was wrapped in a big towel and in her arms for a quick cuddle, Jen whispered, "Let's keep the bubbles a secret, okay?"

"Okay," he said, then ran naked into his room to find some clothes. Jen returned to the kitchen to pour herself another coffee.

The secret didn't last. Carolina could, apparently, smell Cody's crime.

"You little shit!" she yelled. "You stole my bubble bath."

"No," Cody said. "I only borreowed it."

Jen found Carolina towering over Cody, seated on his little wooden chair at the art table, crayons and paper at the ready.

"Oh yeah?" she said. "Well, give it back then, if you *borre-owed* it."

"Carolina," Jen said. "It's okay. He just tried a little bit."

Carolina just looked at Jen and narrowed her eyes. Then she picked up a few of Cody's crayons. "Can I borrow these?"

Cody nodded.

"Thanks," she said, and proceeded to snap each crayon into tiny chunks.

"What the hell?" Jen cried.

"It's eye for an eye," Carolina said. "I see you haven't taught him that one yet."

It was eyes, alright. Cody started bawling and ran to Jen, while Carolina flashed her a scathing look before stomping herself off to her room.

Once she got Cody settled down, with the promise of a brand new sixty-four pack of Crayolas, Jen texted Ben.

> Must go to SSI tonight. A. needs help. Ideas on Cody care?

She didn't wait for a response; she would take Cody to the island if necessary and find a homeschooler to watch him while she let Adrienne save her life.

In a flurry, Jen packed enough clothes for three days, cancelled via email the intro to social media class she was teaching for seniors—a test of their e-savvy—and made a grocery list for Ben that was nearly a complete restocking of the larder. Let him see how much this monster-girl could put away, despite her love of inertia. Could knitting really work up this kind of appetite? Maybe she had worms, or rickets. Carolina hadn't been outside in over a week.

A text came back.

Hope A. is okay. Ask my mother?

Saint Kathy. Cody would be fine for a little while in the house of Godliness, even if he ended up resuming the morbid prayers about dying in the night at bedtime. And *eye for an eye* didn't seem to figure into her messages, luckily—at least none that Jen had heard.

||||||||||||||||||||||||||||

At Long Harbour, Adrienne stood like a figurehead. The wind rippled her honey hair and seemed to smooth her skin back to teenage tautness so that when Jen first saw her she was both comforted and angry. How dare she look so good? She'd probably just had a roll in the hay with Davis, her steadfast, flexible husband. Jen felt as if she hadn't slept in days, and she smelled bad: all the rushing to get Cody to Kathy's and make the last direct ferry had made her sweat.

Adrienne's face showed only gladness to see her, though, so Jen shelved her anger—she was becoming so good at that, it was scary—and opened up her stinky arms for an island hug.

There were some women who lived the child-free life from whom an outsider might glean a touch of nostalgia, yearning, a coating of sadness, a tendency toward baby talk, all because they wanted kids but never had them. Adrienne was not of this camp. She embraced, embodied, the lifestyle (life had a style? Jen joked), and made it seem so natural that even Jen started to believe that parenting was not for everyone, despite her firm notion that there was nothing in life that could teach selflessness or love with quite the same success. Without Cody, she would still be partying, spending her salary (what salary?) on magazines and shoes and gel nails. Without Cody, she would still think of love as another feather in life's plumage, when love was, in fact, the bird itself, or at least the wings that would make the whole being fly.

Adrienne would say, calmly, *But that's what we invented planes for, lovie.*

Jen was jittery from tea and chocolate, and once she sank back into Adrienne's embracing plushy car seats, she felt her heart scolding her.

"If that's bugging you, tell me," Adrienne said, pointing at the flowering vine in a pot between Jen's feet. "I can probably prop it up in the back. I just thought I'd pick one up when I was close to the nursery. I needed another passion flower by the back gate."

"It's fine," Jen said. "There could be a rabid pit bull at my feet, and it'd be fine." Then she started to cry.

"Oh, Jenny," Adrienne said. "You're in rough shape, aren't you?"

The most pressing need was a passion flower for the back gate? Yes, she was.

||||||||||||||||||||||||||||

After a fine dinner of greens, local mead, and lamb popsicles—over which Jen kept imagining the horror on Cody's face if she were to suggest *popsicles*, his favourite food, made of *lamb*, his favourite animal—she was of no use to anyone, so Jen tucked herself into her wrinkle-free linen cloud and slept the sleep of someone who'd been to war.

She woke to the *brrr* of coffee beans. Alone, in a room with windows that, once she pulled back their robes of cream velvet, opened outwards to the sea. Adrienne and Jen had once gone to Europe together and done their share of flinging windows open (and flings); she'd most likely insisted that this sort of window be included in the design. There was something beautiful about that movement, Jen admitted, as she released the smooth metal catch and swept her arms apart as if parting the sea itself, or at least opening her heart a little more.

The waves were little and light, matched by lines of cirrus clouds above—as above, so below. How that phrase had entered Jen's brain—never mind its origin—was a mystery. She loved it when the sky matched her feelings; today it even matched the ocean. Carolina was on the other side of that water—finally far enough away for peace.

She closed the shutters again, then opened them once more. Yes, it felt like a gesture of willingness to receive.

Less than a day on Salt Spring and, already, a full brain switch to Gulf Island speak. That was good—better to start early, because Julianna was going to lay it thickly on her right after lunch.

⫿⫿⫿⫿⫿⫿⫿⫿⫿⫿⫿⫿⫿⫿⫿⫿⫿⫿⫿⫿⫿⫿⫿⫿⫿⫿

Breakfast: local eggs and bacon, tomatoes from the porch. Davis, generous and subtle, discreetly disappeared after they dined. Morning walk: arbutus and their sinewy limbs, starfish the colour of grape gum. Lunch: salad and salmon and homemade bread from a farm stand. Through it all, Jen had talked, and Adrienne had listened, nodded, laughed, hugged, sworn, reassured, and promised that everything would be alright, that she would hear the same from Julianna.

"You're not a bad person for feeling this," Adrienne told her. "You didn't sign up for it."

Amen, sister.

After lunch, Davis drove them to Julianna's place, so they could walk and talk their way back home.

"Welcome, beauties!" Julianna enthused, her wrists doing a sort of rotation to make her hands swirl the air before squishing Adrienne and Jen together in a group embrace.

Once the niceties were out of the way, Julianna led Jen into her reading room, which, ironically, had no books in it at all. In fact, it was a round room, with no windows below the six-foot level, topped by a slanted glass ceiling partially covered by leaves.

"Sit," Julianna suggested, pointing at a pile of hard-looking cushions covered in faded cotton of various colours, atop an Indian rug. Julianna sat on similar cushions across from Jen, and in between them stood a low desk made of wood on which there was a stack of carbon paper and a couple of pens. Jen hadn't seen that kind of paper since high school.

Julianna responded to Jen's thoughts, eerily. "I like to make notes," she said. "I give a set away and keep the other for my records. Technology, like tape recorders, never seems to work for the angels."

"I love it," Jen said. "Back to basics."

"Okay," Julianna said. "Just relax and close your eyes. I'll check in and see who's here today."

The room grew quiet, no sounds from outside entering the space at all; Jen felt like she was tucked inside a turtleneck. After a minute she cracked one eye open, in case she'd missed a cue.

Julianna had her eyes open, but it seemed as if she couldn't see Jen, right across from her. Her face was pale, her brows pulled in, her hands, shaking.

Oh, God, it was bad, Jen thought. Either her angels were ganging up on her, or Julianna had suddenly gotten the flu and was going to vomit all over the desk.

When Julianna spoke it was in a quieter, higher voice.

"You should probably go," she said. "You need to call home as soon as you can."

"What's wrong?" Jen said. "Julianna, what's going on?"

Julianna closed her eyes, then shuddered a little, after which her eyes popped open again. This time, she saw Jen.

"I'm sorry. That's all they want to tell me. You can use the phone in the hall, if you want."

She sat back and straightened her legs out to one side, cracked her ankles by rotating them, then stood up and offered Jen her hand.

Jen took Julianna's cool fingers and let herself be pulled out of the pillow prison.

"It's probably nothing," Julianna said, smiling thinly. "Sometimes the angels can overreact."

Just then, Jen's cellphone vibrated against her hip bone and she jumped as if she'd been lashed. It was Ben's name on the screen.

"What is it?" Jen cried into the phone. "Are you all right?"

No answer came.

"Ben! Are you there?"

"I'm here," he said. "Cody and I are here."

"What's wrong?"

"It's . . . it's Carolina," he said.

Carolina? Not Cody. Relief surged through Jen like embarrassment. It was all she could do not to cry out with the release. "What about Carolina?"

Ben sounded like he was crying. "She's gone."

"Back home? To Regina?"

"No. Just gone. Run away, or I don't know." He *was* crying.

"That's awful," Jen said. "I'll come back as soon as I can."

She joined Julianna and Adrienne on the porch. "I've got to go home," she said.

"Is everything okay?" Adrienne asked.

It was all Jen could do not to say yes.

||||||||||||||||||||||||||||||

Jen settled into her seat on the ferry. She had an hour and a half sailing time to get herself together. All that raced through her head was the proverb from some culture or another wiser than the one they were in: *Be careful what you wish for.*

Jen had not been careful. She'd spent way too many hours imagining a specific teenaged girl, vanishing. But it had been only fantasy, therapy—not sorcery.

Carolina, it seemed, had vanished. Nothing was missing, according to Ben, except her jacket and rubber boots—sensible— and her backpack. No doubt the mountain of wool remained, as did the ragged mess of belongings she'd brought when she moved in.

Ben was beside himself. *What if she's been abducted, or worse?* he'd said on the phone.

Jen didn't think so. Likely she'd just run away. But she told him to call the police anyway.

After a snack and a walk on the outside deck for air, which nicely infused her hair with salt, she had half an hour more to practice her look of devastation.

Another pat phrase came into Jen's head: *I have a vision problem: I don't see that happening.* It was something her older brother used to say when she asked him for a ride, and it always infuriated her.

She did have a vision problem, though. No way could she picture Carolina as part of the family. It was completely unfair to Ben, this obstinacy on her part, and yet, she had no idea about how to bridge the gap.

Ben's nutmeg-haired head was among the first row of greeters at the ferry terminal. He looked ruined. Before she could ask, he said, "Cody's at our place with Mom," then squeezed her so hard she coughed. "I'm so scared," he said.

Jen squeezed back before extracting herself from his grasp and heading out to the parking lot, murmuring things to him that would calm him down. She was no monster. She could support her husband in his time of need.

||||||||||||||||||||||||||||||||

Cody appeared unscathed when Jen arrived home—no mention of the missing Carolina—and wanted to show her his drawings and his new Mad Libs, courtesy of Grandma Kathy. Other than all the names being Biblical and the adjectives words like holy and glorious, they were still pretty funny. *Dogs are glorious animals, and every Moses or Mary should have a blessed pet like God.*

"No calls, then?" Ben asked, when he came in from parking the car.

"No calls, son," Kathy told him. "Would you both like to pray with Cody and me?"

Jen had never seen Ben's face look like that—as if someone had let all the air out of him. It was like the time she tried to pump up her bike tire but ended up allowing all its air out of the valve instead. Prayers from Kathy were meant to make him feel better, weren't they? Instead the idea of them hollowed her poor man right out. Nothing left to do but pray? She knew that meant worst-case scenario to him.

Ben nodded his deflated head. "After I lay down with an ice pack," he said. "I've got a huge headache."

"Of course, honey," Kathy said. "We'll get dinner going."

Cody hadn't eaten yet? Jen swallowed her surprise and watched him choose pancakes from the marginal choices left in the cupboards; clearly Ben had not done the shopping. He dragged a chair up to the counter so he could man the whisk.

|||||||||||||||||||||||||||||||

After dinner they all sat in the living room in a small circle as Kathy led a prayer to St. Christopher. It was the first time Jen had sat on her own couch in months.

Here was the problem: Jen's prayers had already been answered. How could she sit there, gut bursting with Aunt Jemima, and pretend to want Carolina back?

Because: deflated husband. He was nearly flat, a 2-D image of himself.

Because she was not a barbarian.

Because she was secretly afraid that she had manifested this disappearance.

Because she could not get out of the group prayer.

Because maybe manifesting was the same thing as prayer, and despite her denial, she'd been good at it most of her life. Example: she'd been lonely, after dear old Dan knocked her up and skipped town, and although it was the stuff of fantasies, she'd made a list of what she wanted in a lover.

Nowhere on the list had there been a girl named Carolina, but she'd gotten nearly everything else. It was amazing, in fact, when she thought about it, all these years later. She was basically a master manifester. Cody, the wonder kid, had been conceived on her last day of bleeding, when her thoughts had literally just begun to turn toward procreation the week before. And Ben, this empty balloon of a man that she loved sitting beside her, holding his mother's thin hands, bowing his head and mumbling all he could remember of the prayers, mostly a lot of amens, had been the real, live answer to her desires.

She'd made stuff happen! Gratitude swelled within her. But wasn't it better if Jen rested in her secret, sudden awareness? It would have been better for the Jen of six weeks ago, the pre-Carolinian woman who awakened every morning with peace and gratitude percolating through her system, the Jen who'd find a groggy, powdery, fruity-scented Cody in her bed once Ben had left for work.

But that Jen was no more. The current Jen sat between her sad, distressed husband and her suddenly sour-smelling boy—another change since Carolina had arrived, as if having a teen in the house had chemically altered her son, pulled him into early, early onset puberty—and manifested/prayed.

⁝⁝⁝⁝⁝⁝⁝⁝⁝⁝⁝⁝⁝⁝⁝⁝⁝⁝⁝⁝⁝⁝⁝⁝⁝

Two hours of intermittent prayer and silence later, just after the clock chimed ten PM, with Cody was fast asleep against Jen's thighs, the buzzer rang, twice.

Saint Kathy called out *mercy* from where she sat at the kitchen table reading *Chatelaine*. Cody moaned and snuggled in further. Jen got a wave of chills. And Ben leaped up and answered the intercom phone to find Carolina's voice on the other end, saying, *Daddy?* He bolted out the door to greet her in the lobby.

Even Jen hugged the bedraggled girl when she and Ben came in the door. She'd expected to smell booze, smoke, semen, filth, but all she could detect was the scent of night air and a faint trace of spearmint gum.

"I told myself I had to do something big," Carolina said, after she'd been squeezed and offered tea and toast, once a bath had been started. "I wanted to see if I could do it."

"And?" Jen said, feeling a pinch of pride toward the girl, underlined with a slight worry she had overheard her conversations in which she'd said that Carolina was a useless lump.

"It was okay, until it got dark out."

Ben saw the little-girl pout on his daughter's face and responded with another squeeze around her shoulders.

"The Lord was still with you," Kathy said. "You never need to fear."

"Did something happen?" Jen asked. "Are you hurt?"

Her mind leapt to the microbial level, to the under-a-special-light evidence, to delicate, unmentionable tissues, to the possibility that the thundering bathtub would erase both too much and not enough.

"A creepy guy followed me," the girl said. "Down near Granville Island."

"You were all the way down there?" Ben was pale, still shaking.

"I ran to Chapters," she said. "I spent the rest of the night in there until they closed, down in the kids section."

Then, with Julianna-like ability, Jen pictured the water spilling over the tub just seconds before they saw it flowing out from under the bathroom door.

"Oh, shit!" Kathy yelled, and ran toward the bathroom. "I mean, shoot! Benny, get some towels!"

Cody half-woke up and began to whimper, until Jen stroked his head and pulled a blanket over him.

"Jen," Carolina said, sitting down in the chair next to her. "You're a good mom."

And Jen, reflexively, said, "Thank you," before she was able to make her brain and her mouth unite and respond differently. And what should she have said? I'm not *your* mom, or, Yeah, it's true, I'm kicking ass at it, or, It's about time somebody noticed, or, No shit, Sherlock?

Because wasn't this, after all was said and done, what Jen had been trying to achieve—just a little recognition, just a little moment of being seen?

"It's just too bad that Cody is such a little shit," Carolina continued. "It must be because of his bio dad, right? I mean, it can't be my dad's fault."

Jen had been good for so long that it was, like her thank you, ninety-nine percent of the time reflexive. Call and response, do-si-do, wasn't it all a big ol' square dance, and wasn't she a decent, law-abiding, moral-high-grounded woman, even if she didn't call it religion? That left one percent.

The first slap managed to make contact with Carolina's nose, alone, but that didn't matter. Jen's other hand was backup, at the ready, the old one-two, and it hit Carolina's cold, bright face with perfect aim.

The girl yelped like a dog with a caught tail, but Jen had made her own sound—the grunt of a tennis player, serving, the ball in the racquet's sweet spot, bound to be an ace.

What brought Ben and Kathy running, Jen couldn't say for sure, but the satisfaction of both her stinging palm and Carolina's cry of *You bitch!* just as Ben appeared, forced a kind of smirk onto Jen's face—the way a bowl of stones and water in mid-winter forces blooms from bulbs—that she had no chance of disguising from anyone in the room. Julianna had told her to come home, and now she knew why. Jen had powers, just like her. She could make things happen with only her mind.

In fact, right then, Jen had a vision of her perfect blue bowl filled with narcissus bulbs, wrapping their slender roots around ocean-smooth stones so their stems could emerge, then rise to wave their white heads around like peace flags. Just one more thing she would manifest, when the time was right.

Cody started to cry then; two kids crying. And even though Jen was right there, Cody still on her lap, when Ben reached for the boy he raised his arms to be picked up. He burrowed his head into Ben's shoulder, like it was the only safe place for miles.

Mildred MacDonald's right arm was removed on a Saturday, just after lunch. Lunch, in this case, was simply the time of day, given that Millie had eaten nothing since Friday's breakfast of cottage cheese and a hot cross bun. And it was nearly Saturday at dinner before anything else crossed her lips, except for a simple prayer, coming the other way. *Thank the Lord,* she prayed. *I've made it out alive.*

Against everyone's wishes, including the surgeon and her open-minded doctor, she was home from the hospital by the following Friday. On Saturday morning, she felt well enough to make applesauce muffins, and despite the occasional eggshell, she believed they were some of her best. In the afternoon, her daughter-in-law came by to wash, comb, and set her hair, and that night, she worked doggedly on three of the newspaper crosswords she'd missed while she was in Room 233. By Sunday morning, she was tired. A day of rest. But she carried on with her ordinary routine for the Sabbath, which included playing the organ during the eleven o'clock service at the First United Church.

She arrived at ten thirty, as was her custom, to adjust her seat cushions and arrange her arrangements, and she was gladder than ever for the quiet time. Alone in the church, she sat on her bench and inhaled the church's silence and the scent of lemon wood polish. When Millie closed her eyes, she felt a surge of fatigue wash over her, but she ignored it and focused instead on the presence of the Holy Spirit: it was easier to feel its power before the congregation arrived. Sometimes, the pilgrims of the Lord, in all their earthly glory, were easier to appreciate in the abstract.

She began to touch the keys lightly with her one remaining hand. She plucked out the melody to "A Closer Walk with Thee," using her feet to pedal the bass notes in. Then she started in on "Amazing Grace." She gave herself an imaginary pat on the back, which needed no bodily arms at all. It could be done, His will. She could continue as the organist, and no one would be the wiser.

There were only the hundred and ten regular churchgoers to slip it past. Only the eight hundred villagers to hypnotize into forgetting about the accident, most of whom seemed to have heard about it mere moments after the manure spreader caught her shirt and pulled her in. Only the empty sleeve to hide, tucked modestly into her skirt's waistband. And only Jessie Thompson to convince, who at this very moment was barrelling down the aisle in her turquoise jumpsuit, hollering at Millie to get herself home before she fainted on the altar.

Millie smiled, and started to play "How Great Thou Art" as Jessie neared the organ.

"Well, now I've seen everything," Jessie said, standing there, peach nails on hips.

Millie kept playing.

"What in God's name are you thinking, Millie?"

She wasn't thinking, she was praising: *Then sings my soul, my saviour God to Thee, how great Thou art, how great Thou art . . .*

"Reverend Short called me up as soon as he heard," Jessie said. "He asked me if I'd mind taking up the organ for service." She was tugging at her brassiere through the polyester of her one-piece suit, likely to help the buttons stay fastened. "'Mind!' I said. 'It would be an honour.' And I played just fine last week, too, and I was all ready to do the same today. But now, you're here, when you should still be in the hospital, playing like . . . well, playing with only one arm!"

Millie finished the chorus, with feeling, and then came to a slow halt. She laughed, then said, "Not bad for only five fingers, eh?"

"Millie! It's—" Jessie's face couldn't find an expression. "You shouldn't be taxing yourself like this."

"It's better than sitting at home, moping about bad luck." Then Millie remembered Gord. "No offence, Jessie."

Jessie's husband was recovering from a fall off a roof he'd been working on and hadn't seen much improvement. Some said it was drink that caused the fall; others said it was drink that kept him at home these six months later. Millie didn't pry.

Jessie acted as if Millie had said nothing. "Did your doctor okay this?"

Oh, but wasn't the Almighty Doctor another Lord in the minds of some people? An Old Testament God, handing out sentences and commandments along with the drugs. Millie worshipped only one God, and she had a female doctor who didn't interfere with her decisions to take herbal remedies and see the chiropractor when her neck was out.

"No," Millie said. "But I think she'd be fine with it. She tickles the ivories herself."

Millie didn't mention that she was supposed to be on bed rest for at least another week, to speed up healing at the amputation site. She didn't mention the throbbing that had started in her shoulder just a few minutes before Jessie arrived. In all of Millie's sixty-one years, she had never been one to just sit around and complain.

"Well," said Jessie. "If you're gonna play, then what am *I* supposed to do? I'm twenty minutes early."

"Why don't you bring out the choir stands?" Millie suggested, tipping her head toward her missing arm. "That's going to be a bit of a challenge for me now."

Jess stormed off the altar and into the back vestibule, and Millie heard the clatter of metal on metal. The *dammit* that followed was surely meant for more than the music stands. Millie laughed quietly and picked up "Amazing Grace" where she left off. She wasn't going to give up her place on the bench for a minor thing like a missing limb.

It wasn't pretty, the way a Coors Light T-shirt had saved her life. Her Teddy was a good boy, even if he himself was prone to the drink on weekends. But Millie wouldn't complain about this, or anything Teddy might do, ever again, now that he and one of his beer-box T-shirts had come to her rescue. He'd torn that shirt into strips and wrapped her crushed right arm—a stand-in for the skin and muscles that had come away from the bone—and made a tourniquet for the unrelenting blood. Then he'd carried Millie to the truck and drove the ten kilometres into town, since the county ambulance his wife wanted to call was stationed a fifteen-minute ride from their farm: not even an option. Teddy steered around the potholes as best as he could and got her to the hospital in just over ten minutes.

It worked. Although Millie's arm was amputated five inches below the shoulder, if Teddy had not used his T-shirt, Millie would have bled to death on the way. For all those years Teddy had been in Boy Scouts, she said another prayer of thanks to Lord Baden-Powell.

After hauling all twenty music stands out from the back, Jessie tried a different tack.

"Won't your arthritis get worse, Millie? Using one hand all the time?"

Before the accident, Millie had used a support for her right hand while she played on Sundays—rheumatoid arthritis had twisted her fingers so strongly that half of them had dislocated. Even though the left hand's fingers were starting to drift and curl, they were still better off than the right.

Millie finished playing the last notes of the hymn. "Thanks for asking, Jessie. But the Lord has provided me with a blessing.

It was my right hand that plagued me so badly. And now . . . "
Millie's eyes teared up, and she tried to pull a Kleenex from her
blouse with the absent hand before remembering her loss. "He
works in mysterious ways."

Surely even Jessie could appreciate the irony, Millie thought.
But Jessie pressed on. "And your left hand?"

"It's learning to take the lead." Millie chuckled. "I'll probably play
better than ever now, as long as my pedalling feet don't fall asleep."

Millie stood up to shift her cushions. A sudden wave of vertigo
hit her, as if she'd been run into by a burst of strong wind. She
grabbed onto Jessie's arm with her only hand.

"You see?" said Jessie. "You're not up for this at all."

Millie shook her head, weakly. "If I don't move around too
much, I'm as good as new."

IIIIIIIIIIIIIIIIIIIIIIIIIIIIII

The first members to arrive were the Oxtobys, Mrs. in a plum suit
and Mr. with a tartan tie. Mr. Oxtoby called his wife Milady, and
she returned the favour with Milord. They sat in their paid-for
pew, two rows back from the pulpit, with their grandchildren in
descending order by Milady's side. When the littlest ones saw
Millie, they pointed her out.

"Look," said a high little voice. "Mrs. MacDonald's back again."

Millie recognized the voice as belonging to one of the children
who reached into her apron at the after-service luncheons to pull
out stickers and lollipops.

"Good lord," Mrs. Oxtoby said. "I thought she was dead."

Millie smiled and nodded at the family and kept on playing
her hymn. The usual members of the congregation trickled in
and found their usual pews. Millie could hear a buzz spreading
from one pew to the next, but she ignored it all and focused on

the melody at hand (and foot).

She was used to this. The people of her community didn't often share her points of view. They thought she was outlandish, the way she didn't watch television or drink coffee or join in their gossip chains, although she was still on the receiving end of the odd Friendship Cake, adding the ingredients as instructed every day until the batter was bubbling, ready to be divided, and one half given away. Millie liked her simple life on the farm, and she liked worshipping God from the black and whites of her organ keyboard. Why was there anything wrong with that?

The choir filed in and found their seats, followed by Reverend Short. He came from the vestibule, carrying the Bible, smiling blandly but handsomely at the puddle of faces in front of him. The words THE LORD REIGNETH; LET THE EARTH REJOICE hovered over him on the blue ceiling as usual, painted on their golden scroll, but today they seemed to shimmer like sunlight on water. Once he tuned into the processional being played, he gave a wide-eyed glance at the organ. After the last strains of Millie's hymn faded, Reverend Short looked to the organ again.

"Well, my goodness," he said. "What do we have here?"

"Hello, Reverend," Millie said. She could feel Jessie scowling at her from the first pew.

"What a surprise," he said. "Welcome back."

"Thank you," Millie said. "It's good to be here."

He turned his focus back to the murmuring congregation. "Please turn to page 356 in your hymnals and join the choir in singing the opening hymn."

The choir director looked at Millie and nodded.

Teary again, Millie nodded back, and with as much zeal as if she were embarking on a mission to save the world, she began playing "What a Friend We Have in Jesus."

The service carried on as usual, except for the attention Millie was getting. Reverend Short's face held a look of surprise every time he glanced her way.

"Why is Millie's arm gone?" Millie heard a child ask. Yet another asked if that was blood on her shirt, which caused Millie to sneak a peek over to that side of her body. Good Lord, it *was* blood. She ignored it—and the pain, which seemed to be spreading from her shoulder into her neck—and told herself she'd take an extra Advil once the service was through. She just kept on smiling on her organ bench, waiting for her cues.

Eventually, after a rather brief sermon, for which Millie was grateful, the service came to an end. During the closing announcements and prayers, alongside the usual pleas for more volunteers to pour tea at the brunches, Reverend Short thanked the Lord for sparing Millie's life. Then, while the congregation filed out, she played "Just a Closer Walk with Thee," with her eyes closed for focus and pain management. When the hymn was over, she heard her name yet again from the pews.

"Hello, Mildred," Mrs. Davidson called. She'd never been one for nicknames—no one else called her Mildred. "Can we have a word with you, dear?"

There was a group of women waiting at the back of the church. From what she could make out, Candy Jones was there and Ruth Carlson, and among the others, Millie could see the sleeve of a turquoise jumpsuit, peeking out from behind Mrs. Mason's back. Women she had known since she was a newlywed, fresh from one county over and married to a man who had brought her to his farm and made her a farmwife and mother all those years ago.

"Hello," Millie said. "It's so good to see you all."

With considerable effort, she threw her cardigan over her blood-stained shirt and tried to keep her old smile on as she walked toward the last rows of pews, reaching for each row end with her only arm. Maybe they wanted to throw a party for her. Perhaps they would raise some money in her honour, to help cover the cost of the prosthetic arm she'd ordered. Maybe it would be bionic and get her playing better than ever. She'd never be the concert pianist she'd secretly dreamed of becoming back in the day: she had known all along that there was little chance of making the stars line up. No, she'd contented herself with playing for her husband after dinner, a few old favourites they used to dance to, once the children were asleep.

"Welcome back, Millie," Mrs. Mason said.

"Thank you, dear. It's just lovely to be here again."

"What in the Lord's name are you doing back so soon?" Ruth Carlson said. "You should be home resting after such a trauma." Ruth said "trauma" as if it rhymed with "Gramma."

Millie laughed. "You'd think I would like the rest, wouldn't you? But the truth is, I was so jazzed up about being out of the hospital that I couldn't stay at home, especially on a Sunday." Millie sat down, heavily, in the last pew. She was sweating, and her stomach felt a little off.

"But doesn't it hurt?" Mrs. Mason asked.

"Not too bad," Millie replied. "I might get those phantom pains down the road, they say, but right now it's just a little achy." She wiped her forehead with the back of her hand. "I'm just so tickled that I can still play the organ."

The women were silent for a moment. Then Candy spoke up.

"Millie," she said. "That's what we wanted to talk to you about."

From inside her swimming head, Millie looked around at the faces of the United Church Women. None of the faces she had known for all those years were looking her in the eyes now. Or was it *eye*—what was the expression again?

"Since you've had such a mishap," Candy continued, "we think it might be best if you took a little rest from the playing."

"You've had the job a long time," Ruth piped in. "What is it, ten years now?"

That sounded about right. Millie had started playing the organ when June Johansson passed away ten years ago. But June had been playing it for more than twenty. Millie didn't know why she should have to call it quits, especially since she thought she'd sounded better today than she had in years. If only her husband were here to hear it. But three years ago, after thirty-five years of marriage, mostly good, he'd had a heart attack and died on the way to hospital.

That was why she'd needed to learn how to use all that machinery in the barn, including the manure spreader, so she could help her son keep the farm going. And God, via Teddy, had given her a second chance, and although she couldn't use a pitchfork like she used to—and thank the Lord she didn't have to use one right now—one-armed or two, she was still the best organist at the First United Church. But these women, they were saying otherwise.

"It would give someone else a chance to play," Candy said. "It's only fair, we think, to let someone else have a go."

Millie felt more weakness pass over her again, and she leaned her head against the end of the pew.

"You're not well yet," Mrs. Davidson said gently. "Why don't you take some time off? A little R & R, you know. Let the young folks take on the burden."

Millie looked at the group of women, who were beginning to blur into a quilt of colour, patches of pastel and primaries all together.

"It's no burden," she said, quietly.

Mrs. Mason muttered, "It is to the rest of us."

Millie tried to focus on Jessie then, who was emerging from behind Mrs. Mason.

"Is that what you want?" she asked Jessie.

Jessie nodded, her chin held high. "I've wanted to play that organ since I was four years old. I've been practicing every day, and I don't even need to look at the book for some of the hymns!"

As she spoke, Millie could hear Teddy's truck dieseling around the corner on its way to pick her up. Relief flooded through her. Good old Teddy.

"Well, then," Millie said, smiling faintly. "I'll give it some thought." There was no way she was going to give it up that easily, even if Jessie needed the job, as service to the Lord or to keep her from turning against her husband—a way to escape as she had, from the farm, if only for an hour every week.

Millie still needed the escape. She deserved it, didn't she, after all she'd been through? Maybe she would take a poll of the members of the congregation, who'd seemed to enjoy her playing just as much as any other Sunday.

Yes! She would give them a little survey at the door, with boxes beside Jessie's name and her name, somewhere for them to put their checkmarks. Wouldn't it be fun to count up all those checkmarks? Or she could pull out the big guns. If she had to get Reverend Short involved, then that's what she would do. Hadn't he been supportive of her return? Wasn't that approval in his glances all service long? Or was it something else? Did the old devil have a little crush on her? Was he over his wife leaving him for another man in another church in a faraway province? Was he ready to get back on the horse? He was a looker, or must've been, back in his youth.

Good Lord. Her, a minister's wife! What would these ladies say to that?

"Thank you, Millie," Candy said. "We knew you'd come around."

"I'll let you all know," Millie said, faintly, and then stood up and started to walk slowly back down the aisle to the organ, keeping her eyes on the cross that hung behind the pulpit as a target.

"Teddy," she heard Candy say when her son walked into the church in another beer shirt and cut-offs. "I understand you're some kind of hero."

"Nah," he said. "I'm no hero. Youse all would have done what I did."

Millie turned her head and waved at her son.

"I'll just be two shakes, hon," she said.

She looked back toward the front of the church, to get her attention back on track, but she couldn't seem to focus on that big wooden cross. When her right foot hit the edge of the front pew it broke her momentum, but she toppled, falling onto the green carpet, and tried to stick out her missing arm to break her fall. Instead, the carpet met her face, and the stump hit the edge of the altar, and she was down. Down, down, down for another count. If only it were down she'd fallen into, instead of this cheap Berber!

What was that sound? It seemed to belong to a large bird, a kind of squawk, or cry, like from an angry peacock. Was that from her?

On the carpet of the First United, Millie listened as more birds came running down the aisle, chirping behind her son. She pictured their mouths popping open at the sight of her, splayed in front of them, bleeding like a stuck pig. She saw stars and waving colours and the lights moving every which way, and she saw how it was, this church, no more than another place for these women to hold court. She pictured Reverend Short, coming to scold these women for their behaviour, and helping her up; she saw herself as the lady of the church, presiding not only over the organ but over the manse and the first pew and the general gist of everything.

Then, she saw a white shadow, nearby. Was it the Holy Spirit, hovering, ready to take her if she wanted to go?

Was she ready? Was it her time?

When she opened her eyes, there was Teddy, taking off his shirt again, trying to stop the progress of her blood. What was it about her blood? It just seemed to want to escape.

But who was that behind him? Reverend Short? And what was he holding? It looked like a loaf of white bread, ready to be cut up for communion. Or was it a six-pack for Teddy, for all that he'd done?

Teddy should really come to church more often. Next week, she would ask him to stay for the service, to hear how much her playing had improved. And she would buy him a new shirt. I owe him that, at least, Millie thought, as she let her eyes fall shut.

"Millie," Revered Short whispered, right into her ear. "Look what I have for you."

It was all she could do to lift her eyelids, but there, cradled like a newborn in his arms, was her missing limb, with a face like baby Jesus, beaming his unearthly love at them all.

Dear Maddie,

Merry Christmas! And happy 19th birthday. Isn't it good to finally be a grown-up? Able to see the world as it really is? We made it. We're not little kids anymore, lol!

How are you, my friend? Isn't it fun to look back on our lives and see how far we've come? To track the changes, and monitor our growth? That's one thing I've learned at school, among about a billion!!

I'm home for the holidays, and OMG I would LOVE to see you.

I'm sure you are learning so much too, in a totally different way from me. The real world, right? Sometimes the university feels like a whole other dimension (and I'm happy to be in it!), but you're living life for real. How is that baby of yours? I bet she's beautiful, just like you.

In psych class we're learning about personalities and behaviours, patterns and traps, and once you get the lingo, so much of the past can be put into perspective. Every day, I say to myself, if everyone took Psych 100, there would be a lot more harmony in the world.

Please send me some pics! I would totally love to see her. I couldn't find you on Facebook, though. Are you even on there?

It's a complete gong show some days, I know, but it's a good way to keep those special people in our lives.

But anyway, back to what I've been doing. There is so much to tell! Oh Maddie, it's so amazing. I totally get what's happened in my life now. It's like I've been an uncharged cell phone for like, ever, and now, I'm finally plugged in. Like, you know how I used to be afraid of the dark, right? Well, it's no wonder! They call it nyctophobia, and I'm sure half of the world has it, and it usually comes from the power of suggestion. Think about this:

In the great green room there was a telephone, and a red balloon, and a picture of—

That's where the page break is in *Goodnight Moon*. Margaret Wise Brown wants you to imagine what might be in that garish bedroom before the page gets turned. What I want to know is who guesses a bowlful of mush? And what about the mouse? Do you want your baby girl to have rodents in her room? Or even worse, kittens? Have you ever tried to get to sleep with kittens in the room?

That old lady should get out of her rocking chair and put those two kittens outside instead of just whispering "hush." Talk about setting a poor kid up for failure. And don't get me started on the "Goodnight nobody" page. That emptiness is enough to make any child afraid to close their eyes.

You got a copy of this book for your shower, right? I think Maya gave it to you. Well, I'm not saying don't read it to the baby, but you might want to put it away until she's old enough to know better. Otherwise, it'll just make you have to spend hours getting your kid to sleep, like my parents did.

I'm sure they would rather have been doing something else, like spending time on their marriage or something. It wasn't always hunky-dory.

God. I am so sorry. You don't need to hear about a not-perfect marriage when you don't even have a daddy for your baby. How insensitive am I?

This is a Letter of Truth, Maddie. I've got to admit something: I've never told you about what happened that summer I caught a ride to Toronto with your dad. God, that was such a disaster. Not the ride—no, your dad was great, singing country songs and sharing his Swedish berries for the four-hour trip, while I sat there obsessing about that Italian boy I'd met at camp. But when I got to that boy's house, he just stared down at me from the second-floor balcony, as if he didn't know who was at the door. Eventually he came down and talked to me, but it didn't take long for me to figure out that he didn't like me, away from the lake, the tents, the lack of other available and willing girls. His mother looked at me like I was a total whack job.

God, I was embarrassed. That's why I told you I wasn't into him anymore when I got back. I just couldn't admit the truth.

I sobbed all the way home on the bus, and I cried listening to the playlist you and Maya put together for my 16th birthday. I smelled that bandana of his he'd given me at camp. I kept crying.

Then, when I got home, I saw that my father, who was at a conference, had taken the suitcase where I'd hidden a box of Trojans. I'd bought them for the trip but didn't end up taking them. I'd worried too much about an accident, someone going through my luggage and thinking I was a whore. A Catholic whore, no less, because there was that laminated confirmation prayer in my wallet to prove it. Oh, remember how we even took new middle names for confirmation? I chose Veronica, the woman who wiped Jesus's face with a towel on the way to Calvary. Who'd you choose again? I think it was Teresa, right?

Anyway, when my father came home from that conference, he asked me to come into their bedroom.

"Are these yours?" he asked me.

I got red in the face and started crying again.

"I'm not mad at you," he said. "I just didn't think that they were mine."

I felt better for a few minutes, and then it sunk in. My father thought I was having sex and was okay with that. AND . . . my father was having sex with someone who wasn't my mother because why else would there be condoms in a suitcase? For some reason, he wanted me to know.

Then I looked at my poor mother, whom I hated that year (we were forming ourselves, right? It's called Differentiation. It's totally normal), and I felt a mean smile forming. I knew more than she did about what was going on and maybe even about bloody *everything*, and it felt like it was only a matter of time before her world crashed around her like a pane of glass, dropped from above.

The thing was, it didn't. And I was left alone with this information that has smouldered inside me, ever since. Every day, I woke up and wondered if that would be the day she'd find out, but she never did. (More about that later!)

"Why am I telling you this?" you're probably asking. I'm getting there. This is what happened next, right on cue. I established my identity. I balanced what I had with what I wanted to do with it. And all I wanted was to get out of town. I was counting off the days until I could escape to a decent city where there were taxis, buses, streetcars, and different colours of skin. Having fake ID and clear skin and even a car, sure, those were important parts of my development, but I wanted more. I wanted all the things I have now. Like gay friends! International friends! Brown friends! I'm so loving it at school, Maddie, you have no idea.

(Do you ever hear from Maya now? We've lost touch, and I totally want to know how it's all going for her. And what about everyone else in the group? What bad things are they getting up to?)

Although I kept waiting for my parents to break up, I still heard them going at it, as in IT, at least once a week. Maybe Mom opened herself up to forgiveness and secretly renewed her vows. After all, God was watching, or so I thought at the time (I had Religious Delusions). A promise was a promise. Religion is really no guarantee of anything other than another set of rules to follow, or break, is it? Or do you still go to church? I'm thinking you probably don't now. Father Healy can be pretty harsh about straying from the straight and narrow.

I was starting to test what is called fidelity—being faithful to something I believed in or loved despite it not matching what my values were. Although it didn't feel like anything from a textbook: I just needed to get out.

Anyway, you know what happened next. High school was six months away from being over, and you found out you were pregnant. Liam, that idiot, had already dumped you.

Oh, Maddie, I didn't tell you before, but . . . I kissed him. Way before you and he got together—at least a week before. He just had a way with words, and with his tongue (as you know!!), and before I knew it, we were necking on his captain's bed one night while his mother made brownies in the kitchen. I'm so sorry. I know you're not with him now, but still, I should have brought it up before. Is he even in the picture anymore? What a jerk.

I'm really starting to sound like I'm a slut, but you know I'm not, right? I've never even used a condom. I can count on one hand the number of times I danced to "Stairway to Heaven" at those stupid dances, and how many times I wished those lights did not come on at the end, revealing me—and my dance partner— in all our bleary, break-out glory.

So many things look better in the dark. I should never have been afraid of it!

Then your baby arrived just before school was over. That day, when all of us visited you at your house, I know I totally upset you when I didn't want to hold the baby. I know you wanted me to coo over sleepers and blankets and plushy toys, but I just couldn't. I know what it was now: a Coping Mechanism. It might've looked like jealousy to all those other girls, but it wasn't. It might've looked like I didn't care. I did care.

I do care.

She was only a baby, right? Harmless, helpless, an honest mistake. And you seemed okay with all of it: ready to keep her, raise her on your own with your mom's help. But it's so crazy, remembering what I was worried about: what if, just by being around you, some kind of juju rubbed off onto me? What if I got pulled into the vortex of staying in town, helping out, playing auntie, staying true to our friendship? See, I was so certain about my path that I could have nothing interfering. Not even your beautiful baby.

I'm sorry. I was immature.

Anyway, I escaped. When the train arrived, I was the first on board, gaily waving goodbye to my parents (it's totally okay to use that word, you know, as in meaning happiness!). They were both wearing dark sunglasses, but I could tell they were crying. For once, I was not weeping (it's called Mild Dissociation), not until that train slid away, leaving them standing there, arms folded, side by side, watching me go. I was sobbing by the time the next town came into view. And the next.

I'd broken up the family (Survivor Guilt), and I had three days on a train to think it all through. Luckily no one knew me. No one at all (Social Pain, Psychalgia). But that's exactly what I wanted. I just didn't expect it to hurt quite so much.

Enough of the past. I made it west, and everything worked out. I mean, I was free! I was—and still am—taking classes in subjects no one really even talks about back here, like history in art, philosophy, anthropology, and of course, this amazing psych class. My money ran out early in December, though, because I bought a plane ticket to come home for Christmas, so for the past few weeks, I've mostly lived on cheap apples and spaghetti mixed with frozen peas and cream cheese. I'm not complaining. Life is good.

Especially since the next stage in the psychosocial stages list is really the best one, and I think I'm in it!

Love. Figuring out the difference between intimacy and isolation . . . I've met a guy! No living alone for this girl. I mean, we haven't moved in together, nothing like that, but it's just a step in the right direction.

I have a Christmas gift in my luggage from a boy with the strongest chin I've ever seen—a pound of fancy chocolates in a crimson box. Maddie, we've been having so much fun together. He showed me the mountains. I kissed him (and more!) above his mother's kitchen, while she was making bagels, of all things. It is odd that all my good kisses have had mothers cooking in the other room. But I'm not worried—and not complaining.

(Next day, sorry, got sidetracked!)

It's pretty strange being back, seeing the same old things but being totally different inside. And at home too. I thought something was weird here when I first arrived, but my parents told me everything was fine. It was like the space around my parents was full of static electricity.

Then, last night, while I was lying on my Sears catalogue canopy bed, an idea came to me. I was going to interview my parents to get some answers. I would tell them it was for psychology class. Once I got them alone, with me recording it all, I'd ask them to do the Carl Jung test.

This is it. You should totally try it! It won't take long at all. Okay.

Think of and describe:

1. A colour
2. An animal
3. A body of water
4. Being in a white room with no windows or door (describe how you feel!)

Cool, hey? Let me know what you got! I'll put the meanings down below but

DON'T READ AHEAD

Anyway, this morning, before I could do the test, they asked me to sit with them at the table. They poured me a cup of coffee and set warm croissants on the table.

They're selling the house.

The realtor is coming by tomorrow.

They're splitting up and moving into separate condos when the house goes.

They're sorry to drop the bomb, and so close to Christmas. They're sorry. They're sorry.

What do I do, Maddie? My parents are getting a divorce! I asked them, "Was it something I did?" And they said, "Of course not, honey," in these creepy soap opera voices.

Then it hit me. It was true. It was something I *didn't* do that kept them together for this long. I know that if I'd told my mother about those Trojans, my life might have been turned upside down much sooner. I might've split them up way back when.

It's just all too much.

I reacted, and called my boyfriend, and told him that I loved him. But I don't really know what that means! I'm a bit freaked out that I've gone too far. I don't know if I can be with a guy who has such a big chin, and some pretty smelly feet too . . . Maybe you can tell me. You have a baby now, and that takes a lot of love! Did you love Liam when you two, you know . . . made the baby? I can't believe we haven't talked about any of this. I guess I was just focused on marks, and you had all that morning sickness, and then you had to leave school early because of your swelling, wasn't that it? Did you think you'd be with him forever? I'm not sure forever is what I'm looking for, but I just don't know.

I think this holiday is going to suck.

Okay, I better close this epic letter, but before I forget, here are the meanings of that test!

1. The colour is how you see yourself
2. The animal is other people
3. The body of water is your sex life
4. How you feel in the white room with no windows or door is death.

I really want to know what you got! When I took it, my body of water was an ocean. OMG, right? They say they've only discovered a bit of the ocean. It's so huge, it's barely been explored at all.

Anyway, I wanted to write you because, even though we haven't seen each other in six months, you're still my best friend. I could totally call or text, but I'm not sure you'd want to talk to me. And I wanted to send you this little gift for the baby. I hope you don't have any yet! They say that starting flash cards before the age of one can really help a child develop and get ahead in the world. And that's what I want for your sweet baby, Maddie. I only want the best for everyone. There is just too much selfishness in the world.

Hope to see you on Facebook!

Much love from your best friend ever,

Sophia

P.S. If I threw a party, do you think anyone from the old group would come?

P.P.S. Could we hold it at your place, because mine is being sold out from under me?

P.P.P.S. Are you seeing anyone? I totally forgot to ask!! If not, don't worry, your ship will come in any day now. Guys don't care about virginity anymore, right? I mean, having a baby might be a bit of a deterrent, but I bet you're a Yummy Mummy, big time. Plus, if she got your eyes, she'll be an easy sell to any future daddy. Life has a way of working out, Maddie. And oh! I met someone from that university you wanted to go to, and he says it's a total cesspool, so you're not missing anything. Plus, becoming a nurse is so predictable. I know your life is going to be awesome.

P.P.P.P.S. Is Liam still in town?

Falling in love with a foster kid was like falling for a stray dog that's come into the backyard. You weren't supposed to do it. But if anyone told Heidi that, she just didn't listen.

On Boxing Day, they went skiing with Heidi's dad Tom. Owen took a lesson in the morning, on the baby hill, but after lunch, he and Heidi went up the chairlift together to ski the bigger slopes. The snowflakes on his curls looked like miniature fairies.

Heidi's mother had stayed home to sew her a leprechaun costume for the skating show. Instead Tom's work friend, Paula, came along because he'd given her a day pass for Christmas. Paula's husband, home with their little girl, kept phoning her all day long.

Heidi wasn't all that good at skiing, but neither was Paula. Tom kept having to help Paula up. "I'm a mess," she said, more than once. It was true—a giggly mess in a bright peach snow-suit—but Tom didn't seem to mind.

Her father had a soft heart—it was his fault Heidi loved so easily. He worked at Children's Aid, winced when he took out her slivers, stopped into church to light candles for lost and lonely souls. Heidi liked to go and slide the offering into the gold box, choose a few candles, attach a prayer to the flame. The red glass votives pulsed with liquid, beating light, pushing her prayers up beyond the crucifix to where someone was waiting for them, ready to act.

They took their last runs around four o'clock, then hit the road before full darkness fell. Their legs were rubbery, their cheeks rosy, and on the hour-long drive home, they played twenty questions and shared a tin of Paula's gingerbread cookies; the radio blared out oldies, and Paula and Tom sang cheesy harmonies. Heidi counted thirteen smiles appearing on Owen's impish face.

When Paula's cell rang again, just before they got back into the village, she turned it off.

Tom asked, "Checking in again?"

Paula shook her head. "Checking up," she said. "He needs some help."

She shoved the phone into her purse and Tom turned up the radio: "While My Guitar Gently Weeps."

‖‖‖‖‖‖‖‖‖‖‖‖‖‖‖‖‖‖‖‖‖‖‖‖‖

It's nighttime. The kids are waiting in the car in Paula's driveway while Tom helps to take Paula's skis inside.

From the car they can hear snowmobiles zipping around the village, backfiring now and then on the trails between houses. This is the first time Heidi has been alone in the car with Owen, and the air feels like it's made of glitter.

It's been more than a few minutes since her father left them, and she really has to pee. She should have gone at the ski hill, but it takes too long with snowpants.

The radio news is talking about Afghanistan, and after the sports update, Owen says, "This sucks. I'm going to get him."

"No!" Heidi doesn't want to say it; it makes her sound like a baby. "We're supposed to stay in the car and keep it locked."

"What's gonna happen? Nothing ever happens around here."

Her family only has a few rules, and this is one. A boy got abducted from a nearby town, plus once there was a rabid fox by the school. When she tells him this, Owen stays inside but climbs into the driver's seat, changes the station, drums on the steering wheel to the Black Eyed Peas, sings the bad words over the beeps. She's fidgety.

"What's the matter?" he asks.

"I have to—go."

Owen grins. "Number one or two?"

Heidi's face burns. "Number one."

"Go outside."

"No way!"

"I won't look. Just go beside the car." He laughs. "No one will know the yellow snow was you. It's dog central."

"It's okay. He'll come out soon."

Owen sighs. "Why don't I just honk the horn?"

That's also not okay, but Heidi really has to go.

"I guess."

He gives the horn three short blasts. They wait. No one comes. He does it again.

"How could he forget about us?"

"He hasn't." But Heidi is thinking the same thing.

"Then where the hell is he?"

It's been twenty minutes. Owen has just said a semi-bad word about Tom, and she's beginning to feel scared and hungry on top of having to pee.

Then they hear Mozart rise over the modern music. Tom's ringtone.

Owen pulls the phone from the glove box and flips it open. "Hello?"

Heidi's mother's voice. "Owen?"

"Hey, Mrs. Munro—"

"Are you nearly home?"

"Um, we're at Paula's house, and we've been waiting, and—"

"What's going on?"

"I dunno. He just went to carry her skis in."

She pauses. "How long have you been there?"

"Thirty-three minutes."

"Dear God," she says. "Okay. Stay put. I'll be there soon."

Heidi wants to talk to her, to ask if she should just go and get her father. But when she grabs the phone from Owen, she's already hung up.

They're back to waiting.

When Owen suggests they play hangman on the window, Heidi agrees. Her father better not complain about finger-smeared glass after making them wait.

Owen climbs into the back seat again.

"My mother used to do this. She would stop in at a damned bar, and I'd wait in the car for hours."

"This isn't a bar," she says. "And my father never does this. It won't happen again."

Owen needs to know that none of this is normal.

She blows on the glass to fog it up and they play hangman. She needs to pee so bad. They're both freezing. She wants a hug. Every time a car passes, she feels it in her stomach. Not her mother. Not her. Finally, *her*.

But instead of coming over to the car, her mother goes up Paula's porch stairs in her puffy blue coat. She knocks, looks back at them, waves and smiles. After she stands there for another few seconds, peering through the window, she tries the door, then goes inside.

"Three more letters," Owen says, pointing at the window.

"Spaghetti?"

He high fives her. "Nice one."

She watches the clock; four, five, six minutes pass. Her mother isn't coming out, either.

"Let's go in," Owen says. "This is effed up."

But suddenly, her mother appears. She's running down the stairs; there she is, on the snowy lawn, on her knees, screaming, her mother, she's—

Owen reaches over and takes Heidi's hand, and they watch as her mother's hands meet the snow and leave it red. The blood is all down her jacket too, and all at once, the pee Heidi's been holding just won't be held any longer.

There goes Owen's hand.

There goes everything.

‖‖‖‖‖‖‖‖‖‖‖‖‖‖‖‖‖‖‖‖‖‖‖‖‖

Heidi will not imagine a future, but it will come anyway. When her mother tells her what happened, hours later, after her aunt has brought her and Owen home, she will plug her ears, refuse to listen. NO, NO, NO, not this, not her life, no way. Her mother's face will be unrecognizable, she'll be down on her knees—

And she will tell Heidi, and Heidi will hear because fingers are a terrible way to fight sounds. They're only good for one thing, holding Owen's fingers—

But Owen, he'll be gone in the morning, before Heidi is up. He'll need to be removed from the situation—a family now unfit for fostering. And Heidi will cry like a—she will cry, oh, shit, cry like a—she doesn't know what cries like this.

Tom was shot by Paula's husband, who thought Tom was having an affair with Paula, although anyone could've told him they were just friends. Then he turned the gun on Paula, and then himself, thank God, and not the little girl watching *The Lion King* in the family room with her headphones on.

When the house holds just two people, Heidi will cradle her father's leather wallet in her hands and feel embarrassed by the curve in it from his bum. After she opens it, she will find herself in the plastic window, a smiling school picture, hair in ponytails.

Then from behind that photo, Heidi will see another photo's edge. When she slides it out—a second face.

Paula's little girl.

And from then on, Heidi will try—and fail—to separate the tears about her father from those about Owen from those about how, when her father was dying, she was thinking about going pee and spelling *spaghetti* and listening to backfiring skidoos and wondering if Owen's hand in hers meant she was his girlfriend.

On a dark Saturday evening in November, Cassie, Pete, and June Brownley made their way to another family's house for dinner. Alicia, Iain, and Chloe Dawson were new to town and lived just outside of Stevens Falls in a farm-field subdivision, past the truckers' breakfast joint and the John Deere dealership. The houses there, spaced some distance apart compared to the ones in town, seemed naked, self-conscious, the planted maple and birch trees not yet big enough to give privacy to the joined backyards.

Cassie first spotted this new family during the summer, in the Shoppers Drug Mart where she worked, and then, come September, Chloe had ended up in June's classroom. In the schoolyard, Cassie and Alicia had begun to talk. Alicia was a nurse looking for work, and her husband, Iain, had "a portable career" as a writer. By October, dinner invitations had been extended, and although Cassie had offered first, Alicia insisted that Cassie's family come to their place instead.

"Entertaining is my middle name," she'd said that day, lightly touching Cassie's arm when she said it, while they waited for their daughters by the jungle gym. Alicia's fingernails were painted apple green, with a kind of sick shine to them, and they brought to Cassie's mind a counter filled with filo-pastried appetizers, a smiling pig's head, everything glistening dangerously. Despite Alicia's insistence on her only bringing wine, Cassie knew she would pack whole-wheat dinner rolls and a salad, so at least she and June, a picky eater, would have something to eat.

Holidays and dinner parties were danger zones according to her Weight Watchers leader, as if Cassie needed reminding. The calories were ready to gang up on anyone who so much as dared to look at a cheese plate, she announced last meeting, and Cassie had seen the woman beside her visibly wilt.

However, their leader told them, it wasn't about being perfect.

"For victory," she said, "you'll just have to win more battles than you lose."

Cassie was on a winning streak, logging a new low daily, although her leader didn't recommend the scale more than once a week. She couldn't help it; she liked to know where she stood. She was fond of measuring steps as she walked a staircase, counting every one, tapping out an untethered rhythm on her slowly shrinking thighs.

She didn't attend meetings in Stevens Falls, but in the next town over, just for a little more privacy, although she probably didn't need to worry: Stevens Falls was practically half strangers now. It had become a bedroom community for Ottawa, just an hour's drive away.

Cassie hadn't asked Alicia about her motives yet, but her sense was that, in general, the people moving in wanted red-brick history and a return to country livin', a place where the cashiers at the Dollar Store and Tim Hortons knew most people by name and trucks were a part of the family. Above all, they wanted cheaper real estate.

The next town over had been voted "Prettiest Town in Canada" three years running. It was an easy pretty: old, restored limestone buildings and a clock tower, a grassy, treed park on either side of a meandering river, with cute little bridges to cross and leave all your troubles behind. Cassie liked to walk through the park a couple of times before her meetings, one last blast before weigh-in, casting off her old self as she went.

A river also ran down the middle of Stevens Falls, but it would never win the award. It was a railway town, with more than a few abandoned warehouses and factories and a reputation for bar fights and youth gangs. And despite its proximity to the capital, it had always seemed to operate by a different set of rules. Yet, she and Pete liked their rough-around-the-edges town and their side-street house, red-bricked and white-porched, a hundred years old. It was unpretentious. It was home.

||||||||||||||||||||||||||||||

The Dawsons' doorbell played "Jingle Bells" although Christmas was still weeks away. After a shy hello at the beige-sided split-level's front door, young Chloe took June by the hand and led her away, proclaiming, "The kingdom awaits!"

Cassie had never met Iain before. She fumbled the kiss-on-the-cheek greeting he gave her so that their lips touched. Alicia, luckily, offered only a hug.

"Leave your shoes on," she told them. "The floors are freezing."

Pete disobeyed her; he'd gone to a lot of trouble to find matching socks that didn't have holes, but Cassie left her heels on as instructed. Heels could take a good five pounds off a silhouette.

Alicia's feet were encased in matted-looking wool slippers, but Iain wore soft leather boots with skinny laces. Cassie's imagination leapt to life: she pictured Alicia untying them with her green-tipped fingers, or maybe even her little white teeth. Everything about Iain screamed urban life, from his purple dress shirt and non-denim jeans to his sculpted hair and the way he spoke with a lifted chin. When Cassie tried to picture herself undoing Pete's work boots by mouth, she nearly laughed out loud.

These people wouldn't know it to look at him, but scruffy-headed and thick-shouldered Pete was quite intelligent. She had to stop herself from saying so, like a dog owner who calls out, *Don't worry, he's friendly!* even when the dog's got his muddy paws on a person's chest. But was furniture-builder Pete all that friendly? He may have come from the prettiest town, but his mouth could spit out some rather unpretty things. Cassie hoped he would mind his hockey-player tongue tonight.

Iain accepted Cassie's bottle of Zinfandel and poured her a glass while she looked at the huge photo on the wall, the smiling family sporting bright sarongs and messy hair.

"Bali," Alicia said, when she saw her studying it. "Ever been?"

Cassie shook her head. "If it's not in Florida, we haven't been there."

Alicia smiled and nodded. "Florida's nice. Why don't we graze a bit?"

Cassie and Pete sat on the bar stools by the kitchen island and began to sample the appetizers. The crackers under the cheese had the consistency of dried soap scum, and the cheese spread was light and creamy, but it fizzed a bit when it met her tongue, and what was that burning aftertaste, sharp as a fingernail on the roof of her mouth? Chili flakes? Pepper?

"It's a sort of crushed insect from South America," Iain explained. Cassie's face was burning. "We brought back a fine selection from our journey last winter," he continued. "I hope it's not too spicy."

"How interesting," Cassie said. Her mouth had begun to water the way it did during the flu.

The other appetizer was some sort of orange fruit with its leafy wings still attached, a bunch of them gathered around a dish that held a tarry dip. "Have a bit of marmite," Iain urged them both. "Something from my parents' homeland."

"Put some shrimp on the barbie, mate," Pete said, after which Iain smiled coldly. It was the only Australian thing Pete knew to say.

Cassie wanted nothing more than a simple shrimp ring with a no-points cocktail sauce to dip their bottom-feeding bottoms into. She ate one of the flying fruits. Although they were tart, they were more recognizably digestible than anything else on the table. She took three more.

In between smiles and bursts of inane small talk, she gulped her wine and uncrossed her raspy, pantyhosed legs so she wouldn't fall off her stool. Bar stools were not meant for ladies. She felt nothing like a lady, anyway—more like a buzzard perched beside the counter. A hungry, sad bird of prey with nothing to eat in sight. Why had she dressed up so much?

Pete took another Molson from Iain. Iain held up the bottle of wine and raised his eyebrows at her. Was more wine a good idea? She forgot how many points per glass. And who was driving home? Before she could figure out her answers, Iain topped up her glass.

"I love your hair," Alicia said. "How do you get that kind of volume?"

Cassie giggled. "My little secret. Next time you're in the store, I'll let you in on it."

She was used to this kind of compliment; Cassie still looked like the Mary Kay lady she used to be, back in the late nineties, when she'd wanted more money than her cashier's wage at the Independent Grocers had offered. She'd been so young and hopeful back then, pencilling the life back into the eyes of the older women of Stevens Falls, following a script of compliments that worked its magic every time. She tried to believe she was making a difference in their lives, that the women would reorder once their favourite magical elixirs ran out, but then the Shoppers Drug Mart came to town, and that was that. She got a job at the makeup counter, worked up to beauty boutique manager within a year, and now did most of the hiring and firing. She knew every product on the shelves in every department.

Pete and Iain had begun talking sports, sans hockey. Cassie felt a small jolt of pride that Pete could talk about Federer and FIFA without making a joke.

Alicia shrugged her shoulders. "I don't know what the hell they're talking about. Would you like to see our Hall of Shame?"

"Sure," Cassie said, all smiles and confusion, and Alicia took her arm and led her down the hallway.

"A different trip each frame," she said, proudly. "My God, look how skinny we were before kids."

In the first set of pictures, a younger, tanned version of Iain and Alicia grinned out at them, poolside and on the beach, except for the one where they were nearly naked, looking at each other, foreheads touching.

"Honeymoon?" Cassie asked.

"No, that was the trip where we met. Thailand." Alicia made a hooting noise. "It's a wonder we have any pictures with us wearing clothes."

Cassie laughed a bit and quickly moved on to the next one. There they were, looking down at an infant Chloe; another showed baby Chloe smiling, and a third captured her holding a dandelion in her little toddler hand.

"Adorable," Cassie said. Truthfully, Chloe looked starved and tentative, but who was she to judge? June had been an unusually beautiful baby, with her Shirley Temple curls and big dimply grin.

"Yeah," Alicia said. "The good old days."

Cassie suddenly felt like something had come to life in her stomach, so she quickly excused herself and went to the bathroom. She sat on the toilet and waited for something worse to follow. Could she get some kind of traveller's bug just by eating those weird foods? Could they rehydrate in her gut?

The bigger question was, where was she? Cassie felt completely lost. She did not recognize the soaps or creams in there, nor did she recognize the scents wafting out of the oven or the toys strewn about the place. Alicia and Iain seemed nice enough, but they didn't exactly have a lot of common ground with her and Pete. Maybe it was the pink wine talking, but she was starting to feel like this house was completely foreign, as if a pod from a distant planet had dropped into this subdivision, and the locals were expected to welcome the newcomers and say nothing about their third hands, their strange way of talking, their silvery skin.

IIIIIIIIIIIIIIIIIIIIIIIIIIIIIIII

Dinner eventually came: some kind of bony fish, a bitter grain flecked with slimy whole garlic buds, and a bowlful of unadorned boiled kale. Both girls flatly refused all of that and instead grabbed two buns each and a decoration of lettuce and cucumber, upon which they both poured half a cupful of Thousand Island Lite dressing.

"You're our first guests!" Alicia proclaimed, raising her glass. "To new friends."

They all clinked and repeated the toast. Cassie and Pete both reached for the bun basket at the same time.

After they dug into their meals with varying degrees of enthusiasm, Iain started up the conversation.

"Peter, we're in the market for an armoire," he said. "What kind of wood do you work in?"

Pete shrugged. "Armoire, you're talking maple or oak, if you want it to last. But we can do pine too. All depends on what kind of coin you're willing to part with."

Iain nodded. "Do you have examples online?"

"Nope. No website. We're strictly in person, in cash." Pete half-smiled—it was a point of pride for him, staying off the web. "Plus, we're backed up about three months right now, so you're gonna have to wait a bit."

"Wow," Alicia said, apparently impressed. "That's a good position to be in."

Cassie swore she saw her wink at Pete. Ha! *Position.*

After dinner, Iain sat on the lean, cream sofa and held his own hands, looking like a priest or an odd uncle. He was done drinking, it seemed—a drink being the most appropriate hand-held object after dinner. Or before dinner. Or during dinner, especially when the food had not been all that edible, other than the chocolate ice cream—totally worth the eight points—for dessert. But he didn't even have a cup of tea. Had anyone offered tea?

Cassie was holding her hand-blown wine glass, rubbing the charm—a wire ring with a blue bead on it—up and down the stem, trying not to empty it as quickly as she wanted because somehow the bottle was over half gone. Pete gave her the look. The stem was not a penis, nothing like a penis, and yet it had to remind them all of a penis, with her gliding that hoop up and down the thick glass stalk. She couldn't stop. It was keeping her from jumping up and running into the bathroom to escape, again, where she would try not to look in the cabinets, again, and fail. *Had* Alicia winked at her husband?

Iain was describing their former life in the city. "All Volvos with bumper stickers. Greenpeace and baby seal love and Save the Earth." He shook his head. "We wanted real," he said, gesturing at the dark windows. "Gritty. Closer to the actual land, rather than just hot air about it."

"Salt of the earth," Cassie said, because if she didn't say it, somebody would, and then she would have to hide her annoyance.

"Exactly!" Alicia said. "Real raccoons, not back-alley trash ones."

"We got those too," Pete said. "You'll have them around here, for sure."

"You know what we mean, though," Iain said. "Once you travel to other countries, where people live closer to the land, you realize how false a life can be."

Pete burped quietly behind a fist. "Can you smell the 3M plant from here? I hear it gets bad when the wind's blowing from the south."

Cassie laugh-hiccupped, but no one joined her. That was her Pete, always telling it like it was. They were both just so tired of people believing that small-town living was country living. It wasn't. It was closer to city life than any city person knew, even once they moved, because they still had their notions, their filters of rustic gold through which they saw—and filmed and posted about on social media—their new, simpler life.

Well, Cassie had an urban setting on her makeup mirror, and she had no trouble using it. She could carve a decent cheekbone into a face that lacked any and send that woman on her way to see a concert in Ottawa. In fact, she and Pete drove into the city at least four times a year, not including the Christmas shopping trips; it was only an hour away, after all. She knew the people there were made of the same flesh and blood as the townspeople. In truth, they were becoming one and the same, now that the town was filling up with them.

She was surprised that Iain and Alicia had chosen this sub-division over an old house like theirs. Then, the wine made her say so, out loud.

Alicia and Iain looked at each other. He nodded.

Alicia said, "Iain has a sort of—aversion." She paused. "To the colour of bricks. So we had to steer clear of the old ones."

Cassie looked at Iain. What was this man doing on earth? Where had he come from?

"I feel ill, you see," he said. "When I see rust-coloured things. I've tried to work it out with my therapist, but we just can't seem to clear it from my brain."

"Someone clock you with a brick once?" Pete asked.

Iain shook his delicate head. "Nothing like that. I just can't explain it, but my body reacts."

Cassie looked around the high-ceilinged room. Not a trace of terra cotta, rust, maroon, or anything close to red—everything was blue, green, white, or blonde. It was like being inside an ice cube.

Just then the girls pranced into the room, dressed like princesses, wielding sparkly wands.

"We're here to turn you into frogs!" June shouted.

"And pumpkins!" Chloe added.

"Okay!" Cassie said, smiling at the girls and their obvious delight.

Alicia was not smiling at the girls, and neither was Iain.

"Chloe," Alicia said, harshly. "We asked you to stop this."

The girl aimed her wand tip squarely at Alicia's lips. "Silence, pumpkin! A squash cannot speak."

"Well, a magical one can," June said.

"She's not magical," Chloe said. "She's just an ordinary old pumpkin."

"Now, Chloe," Iain said. "Your mother has asked you—"

"Quiet, frog! You're only allowed to croak."

Iain sighed, closed his mouth, and drooped against the back of the sofa, silent.

Cassie sat forward in her chair and drained her glass. This occurred on a daily basis at home, and Cassie had gotten very good at ribbitting through meals in front of a satisfied young tyrant. Pete didn't exactly play along, but he didn't seem to mind. Usually he just said, "Is that right?" and carried on with his meal, his TV watching, his shop-cleaning.

"Those are powerful wands, girls," Cassie said.

The girls both nodded. "Mommy," June said. "You're a . . . you're a . . . " Her round face tightened with concentration.

"She looks like the queen," Chloe said. "With her big hair."

"But she doesn't have a crown," June said. Then she brightened up. "You're a queen bee!" she cried and brandished her wand around Cassie's head. "Buzz, bee! Buzz!"

And Cassie buzzed like a good little bee.

That left Pete. He was holding a green silk pillow in front of his face, and Cassie hoped he wouldn't leave fingerprints—or even worse, a faceprint—on its fragile surface.

"You can't hide from us," Chloe said to him. She poked her wand right into the pillow, hard. "Princess June, should we make him something . . . evil?" At this she narrowed her eyes and swung her head around in perfect mimicry of Mr. Burns from *The Simpsons*. Were they really letting her watch that show?

"Yes!" June said. "An evil cat."

"A cat?" Chloe asked. "That's not very evil."

"My cat is. She scratches me all the time." June held out her arm to display her wounds. Of course, she didn't share that she regularly tormented the poor animal by playing dress-up and laundry basket circus.

Chloe shrugged. "Okay. An evil cat, then. With wings!"

She tapped the top of Pete's head lightly with the wand, and it was done. They were all new creatures, stuck watching these glittering, puff-sleeved girls as they giggled and danced away.

For some reason, Alicia looked close to tears, and Iain had his eyes closed. Pete meowed, faintly, which made Cassie snicker until she turned it into a buzz.

Then, thirty awkward seconds later, as if he'd been plugged in to recharge, Iain came back to life. He raised his index finger in front of his mouth to keep them hushed, stood up, then whispered, "Come with me."

He walked to the vestibule where their coats and boots were waiting, and for a second Cassie thought they were all going to leave. Instead he opened a door to reveal a set of beige-carpeted stairs leading downward. Quietly, the four of them padded below.

"That nonsense doesn't work down here," Iain said.

"I'm sorry about that," Alicia said. "Iain, will you please go up and talk to her?"

He shook his head. "It's okay, honey. I'll chat with her when June isn't here."

Alicia turned to Cassie and Pete. "We've been having trouble with Chloe's, um, sense of reality. It's a little—off—so we're trying to get her to cut down on the imaginary play."

"Huh," Pete said. "Isn't that normal?"

"Not twenty-four-seven," Alicia said. "I can't even speak in my own house anymore. She keeps muting me."

"I want to show you something," Iain said from across the room, in front of a closed door. He was grinning, and Cassie's imagination kicked into gear again: she saw herself and Pete being locked up down here, then eventually, after a vague period of torture, sexual or otherwise, hanging from their necks. Why had all her thoughts turned macabre here? She pushed the image down and followed Pete over to the door. What had those crushed bugs *done* to her?

"This is my passion," Iain said, and he opened the door to reveal a huge room, with a miniature 3-D world on the floor and a fleet of small, perfectly spaced plastic vehicles parked in a row.

"Whoa," Pete said. "RC heaven."

"What does that mean?" Cassie asked.

"Radio control, or remote," Iain said. "These are radio. No wires. Kind of like . . . magic." He grinned again. His teeth were long and slender, more like toes than teeth.

Cassie looked around to see how Alicia felt about all of this, but she was still across the room, on her knees, cleaning up Popsicle sticks and pom-poms. Cassie left the guys to the RC room, Pete's face more lit up than it had been all evening.

And what the heck? Alicia was crying behind her stringy hair.

"Kids are messy, aren't they?" Cassie said. "June's art corner is an absolute pigsty."

"All I do is clean up this goddamned place," Alicia said. "She won't even go outside, because she's afraid of the 'wilderness,' as she calls it. She only wants to make believe and put me under spells."

Cassie had to turn her face away from Alicia. It was wrong to laugh. Alicia was trapped in the fake burbs with a stuck-up man who played with toys and a tiny princess who clearly had not been put in her place, ever. That was an old-fashioned notion, maybe, but had June suffered by understanding the rules of their family? Not a bit.

"What about enrolling her in Brownies? They make nature fun." God, she was going to bust a gut listening to herself. "And when they turn into Girl Guides, they get to do a lot of camping."

"Chloe, a Girl Guide?" Alicia laughed bitterly. "Not a chance."

"It's less—military—than it used to be," Cassie said. "Like when we were kids."

"I was never a Girl Guide. I was never anything."

Odd, Cassie thought. Or maybe that explained some things. "Where'd you grow up?"

"Ottawa, born and bred," Alicia said. "My parents can hardly bring themselves to visit us out here. They never pictured me as a country girl, and to be honest, neither did I." She lay down on the shaggy brown carpet and looked up, then pointed at the ceiling. Sparkles surrounded pot lights in a stucco whip. "I mean, we've literally gone back in time here. I never wanted to be a seventies housewife, I really didn't."

Cassie sat down beside her.

"Why are you really here, then?" She'd been bolder, more forthright than she usually was all night, so why stop now?

Alicia looked up at her in the split-level silence, which wasn't silent in the least. They could hear a collection of foot thumps above them, an electric whine from the man cave. She looked like a woman-costumed girl, with a pouty frown.

"You'll think it's dumb."

"No."

"It *is* dumb." She sat up again.

"Try me."

Alicia started to stack the Popsicle sticks into piles of five. Her once-fancy nails were now chipped, hands red and chapped, as if she'd been doing dishes for weeks in scalding water.

"It's Iain," she said. "He needed space for his hobby." Alicia put air quotes around *hobby*.

"Ah," Cassie said. "And what is that?"

"His fucking toys! That room is where he spends all his time, other than when he's dashing off a little article." She swept the sticks into messiness again. "I don't know if I can last, Cassie. I'm not built for this."

The guys were hooting and cheering above the whining, high-pitched sound of racing cars. They moved for this?

"Any leads on a job yet?" Cassie asked.

Alicia laughed, mirthlessly. "Nope. No openings for nurses around here, or so they keep telling me, even at the care homes." Then she sighed. "They told me to apply as a pharmacy assistant."

Cassie's mother's voice piped up in her head: *Maybe it's your attitude that's holding you back, missy. You know that sugar catches more flies than vinegar.* If Cassie herself gave Alicia an honest appraisal—a professional opinion—she'd say that it might be more about presentation. A bit of mascara, a little blush, lipstick: that would make her appear more likeable. Some people didn't need much help, didn't look raw and burnt out like Cassie did without makeup—and Alicia was one of the lucky ones—but then, just to be content with that, not even try to enhance the natural beauty? This was where the tragedy was. This was where Cassie could work her own magic.

"Alicia," Cassie said, leaning in closer to her. "I've got an idea. Something to cheer you up."

"More wine?"

Cassie shook her head. "Better. Can we leave the girls here with the guys for a little while? There's somewhere I want to take you."

"Hell, yes." She yelled Iain's name. When he didn't answer, she ran over to his room and kicked on the door to knock. "Iain!" she called without opening it. "You're in charge now. The ladies are going out."

Before they left the house, Cassie followed Alicia upstairs to check on the girls. Alicia put her ear against Chloe's bedroom door and furrowed her untweezed brows before opening the door.

The girls were under the purple satin bedspread, their princess dresses—and a bunch of other outfits—in piles all around the room.

"What are you doing?" Alicia asked.

"Snuggling," Chloe said. "We're playing married."

June's face was pink as she moved to the edge of the bed, holding the quilt up against her chin. Caught, naked. Cassie didn't know what to do.

"Dear God," Alicia said. "Put your clothes on, please, and go play downstairs in the rec room. Your father's in charge now."

"Where are you going?" Chloe asked.

"Out," Alicia said. "Come on, now."

Cassie had to say something. "June, do what Alicia said, and listen to your father while we're gone. And put your dress back on, this instant."

"But where are you going?" Chloe whined.

"Just out for a drive," Cassie offered. "We won't be long." She turned around quickly and bumped into the doorframe, then into Alicia, and giggled her apologies.

Alicia suggested a coffee before they left. "Just to be on the safe side."

Cassie didn't argue. She hadn't downed the whole bottle of wine herself, had she? Either way, what she'd imbibed hadn't had much food to temper it.

"Sorry about that stuff in the bedroom," Alicia said, when they reached the kitchen.

"Oh, it's harmless," Cassie said. "Exploring . . . is part of growing up."

"You're probably right. I tend to overthink these things. Sometimes it's all just too much for me."

They began to tidy up the dinner dishes while the coffee brewed. "It's no easy job, is it?" Cassie said. "This parenting gig."

"I'm just so embarrassed," Alicia said. "I don't know what's going on with Chloe. I honestly don't."

"It might have been June's idea, you know. Don't sweat it. And didn't you ever, you know, mess around with friends like that?"

Alicia stopped rummaging for containers to house the left-overs. "Did you?"

Cassie felt a blush rising. "Just a bit. Nothing over the top."

"Tell me!" Alicia said. She'd begun loading the dishwasher. "This is supposed to be Iain's job, but what the hell. We're waiting for java. Now what happened?"

"Well, the first time was on a sleepover, with two other girls, when I was twelve."

"No!"

"It wasn't a big deal, really. We, umm, felt each other up, and then it never happened again."

In truth she hadn't even liked the girls, both named Amanda. She had not been able to say no to the sleepover, since her mother was friends with one of their mothers, and what excuse did she ever have, to not go? The truth was, Cassie had been asked by both Amandas—earlier in the year, when they'd been fighting fiercely—about joining their little gangs, and she had said no to both, that she couldn't choose. But there she was, sandwiched on a pull-out couch, having her hands grabbed and moved to open upon one budding breast, then another, and her own chest—still barely rippled—felt up by four Amanda hands.

"And the second?"

Alicia seemed to be really getting into this. Or was it just the hot water making her face flushed?

"Oh, well, I was at, umm, Guide camp."

"Aha! And you said that Girl Guides would be good for Chloe."

Cassie laughed. "It wasn't a huge deal."

"Then why are you blushing, girlfriend?"

Girlfriend. No one had ever called her that. "It's warm in here."

Alicia leered. "Go on, then. Spill it."

"I just—" How much of this should she tell her? No one else in the world knew of it, except the other girl, Barbara, who'd been from Toronto. "I wasn't a Girl Guide, I was the level after that. A Pathfinder."

"So how old?"

"Thirteen, I think." Barbara was a year older, and her breasts had fully settled in, along with pubic hair and a desire for exploring whatever Cassie would let her.

"We were figuring out what made us feel good, that's all. Late at night, we'd sneak out of our cabin and go swimming together, or crawl under the flipped-over canoes."

One of them pretended to be a boy, on top, and the other stayed beneath, both wriggling, rubbing and kissing until the pleasure came. It was all kinds of wrong, and dangerous, and astonishing.

"Damn, Cassie," Alicia said. "You're full of surprises, aren't you?"

She laughed. "Speaking of, we should get going soon, shouldn't we?"

"You're not going to, you know, try something kinky on me, are you?"

"God, no. I'm not—all of that was just kids' stuff. I'm into men, one hundred percent."

And she was. But she could feel a faint throbbing in her crotch now, her pantyhose a little damp at the top of her thighs.

|||||||||||||||||||||||||||||||

As soon as they were in the car, Cassie at the wheel, Alicia pulled out her phone. "I'm switching this to the 'don't give a shit' setting."

"I don't even have a phone," Cassie said. "So I guess I'm always on that setting."

"Amen, sister! I don't care where you're taking me. I'm just happy to be out."

"It's not far," Cassie said. "We're just gonna have a little fun."

Alicia turned up the radio, and Katy Perry sang to them about being young forever, and for a second it felt like a teenage dream, two friends out together, in the dark, going anywhere they wanted.

Cassie remembered Alicia's unhappy face in the basement, cleaning up. It was true: parenting *was* hard some days. Maybe they had more in common than she wanted to believe.

Cassie had also hoped for escape. She'd been on the path to higher education and an unknown but predictable future, ready to leave Stevens Falls and never look back, about to extend her young life like a mechanical arm and grab onto whatever she could reach.

Then, the winter before high school was over, her mother changed. Not a turn for the worse, but for the worst, in the form of a particularly aggressive form of MS, and like a character in an Alice Munro story, Cassie changed her plans.

She could have chosen to attend school nearby, with two college towns an hour's drive away, but that wasn't going to work with her mother's needs, and besides, what could compete with the practical education she was receiving at home? Within months, her mother's body had transformed from a reliable machine that needed little maintenance into a rusting, unpredictable vehicle she just wanted to leave in a ditch. Or so it appeared to Cassie: apparently her mother had been ignoring symptoms for at least a year.

Cassie's father was long gone by this point, having had his fill of family goodness around her eighth birthday, opting for oil work out west, where he sent money from and called it fathering. She didn't miss him much, except when it became her job to clean out the fireplace, stack wood, catch spiders and mice, and eventually, help her mother into her wheelchair and out again, numerous times a day.

She met Pete at a party the summer after the year she should have gone away and come back, transformed, to tell the tales. Someone had ripped the pedestal sink from the wall in the house where the party was raging, and the thing began to fountain. Instead of yelling and grabbing towels, Pete was the one who ran to find the main water valve and shut it off.

They started dating later that week and were married a couple of years later. Her mother lived with them until June was born, then moved into extended care.

She'd meant to reach further than the next town over, but that was fate for you. You couldn't always plan the path to your happiness. And wasn't she happy, doing the things women in this town did, marrying and raising a child with a decent, practical man? Even if having only one child, just as her mother had done, was seen as a little odd, she was content enough. In a settled kind of groove, anyway. Sure, she had a job with a ceiling she'd already touched, and her mother's care facility barely seemed to meet her needs, and her husband, while having ample plumbing and other hands-on skills, lacked aplomb in most situations, but still. It was her good life, and she would never ask for anything else, and she relayed all of this to Alicia as they sipped coffee from their to-go mugs while they drove into town.

When they were only a few minutes from the store, two fire trucks, an ambulance, and a police car raced past, sirens screaming, then turned down the old quarry side road.

"That doesn't look good," Cassie said, quietly, but her heart was pounding: how much wine had she consumed, and would they make her walk a line?

Alicia looked at her. "You know anyone out that way?"

"Sure."

Of course she knew people out there, and in every other direction too. But Cassie wasn't worried about them, per se. It was just a rare sight to see all those emergency vehicles, all at once.

"Let's follow them!" Alicia said. "I've never done that."

"What, chase an ambulance?"

"Yeah!"

Cassie slowed down but didn't turn the car around. Truth be told, her guts were roiling at the idea of bodies and wreckage, even if Alicia was supposed to be a nurse. She switched the radio from pop to the local soft rock and country station and kept driving toward town.

"Let's see if they say anything on here."

Had she overshared tonight? Everyone else in her life already knew most of the things she'd told Alicia, and there was something about telling a stranger your life story to make a person feel, well, particular. Not just like everyone else in this small community. Talking to another woman, heart to heart: Cassie hadn't really done this since her early twenties. And even if Alicia had peculiar taste and a strange parenting style, it all made the evening felt a bit less like a visit to an alien planet.

Sure enough, after the Roto-Rooter commercial, the news said there'd been reports of a plane crash in the area, out near the old quarry.

"Oh, my God!" Alicia said. "That's wild! We should check it out!"

A plane crash? Here? There were no direct flight paths overhead, that she knew of, and no runways for miles. Cassie felt a wave of weakness come over her, again imagining blood and damage.

"It's terrible. But no. I don't think we should go. We'd probably just get in the way."

"I guess you're right," Alicia said, looking out into the black night. "So, what exciting location are you taking me to?"

"Well . . ." Cassie laughed, lightly, although she was still thinking of the crash. "I wanted to surprise you with something at the store. We'll have the place to ourselves, and I thought I would give you a makeover, if you wanted me to."

"Oh, wow, Cassie," Alicia said, slowly. "That's very sweet of you."

"Oh, it's nothing. You had us for dinner, remember?"

"Wait. You think I need a makeover?"

"No, no," Cassie said, but if it hadn't been dark out, her red-hot face would have betrayed her. "I just thought it would be fun. Something to get us out of the house."

"And thank God for that. But then what? After you doll me up? What am I supposed to do with a gorgeous face around here?" She laughed and pushed Cassie's shoulder. "Are you sure you're not trying to seduce me?"

"Hehe. No, you're safe with me." And she was. The arousal before—now vanished—had been completely memory-based.

Alicia was quiet for a second. "I tell you what. Let's do it, on the condition that we go out for a drink after."

"I'm in," Cassie said. "And you're okay, you know, about not going to see the plane?"

"What plane?" She slapped Cassie's thigh. "It's girl time."

||||||||||||||||||||||||||||||||

At Shoppers, while Cassie set up, Alicia skipped through the aisles testing lotion and perfume samples, then ripped open a bag of cheese puffs and had two of them stuck up her nose when she came back to Cassie's station. Who *was* this woman?

When they'd walked into the store, Cassie was all too aware that they were in the public eye, store lights announcing them to the dark parking lot and the road beyond. It wasn't unusual for her to work late sometimes, but if anyone asked, she would say inventory, or emergency for her daughter. Cough syrup, or maybe something of a more delicate nature—suppositories. Yes, that would shut them up.

Now, though, with Alicia gone feral, Cassie decided to move the whole production into the staff room and cut the front lights. Contain the potential damage.

"There's a radio back there," Cassie said, to lure Alicia in. "So we can listen to the news."

"Why the hell would we do that?"

She'd forgotten about the crash already?

"Come on," Cassie said. "I need running water."

Alicia grabbed a big Toblerone and followed Cassie. "I'm keeping track, you know. I'll give you the money."

"Sounds good," Cassie said. "I'll ring it all in tomorrow."

In the staff room, Cassie turned the store lights back to their usual half-brightness—the company's prescription to deter thieves—and set things up at the lunch table.

"Come, your majesty, sit in this throne," Cassie said.

Alicia scowled. "I've had enough princess bullshit, thanks."

"Oops. Get your butt into my beauty machine," she said. "Is that better?"

She was going to start from scratch, if Alicia would let her. Do a mini facial to freshen things up before the serious application of cosmetics began. "Have you ever had a full face done?"

"Yeah," Alicia said. "My wedding day. I looked like a peach-faced hooker."

"Even in the photos? Sometimes the orange tones translate well to film."

"Especially in the photos. I had to get them retouched before anyone else got a look at them. That's why you didn't see any on the walls at home. They're pretty gruesome."

Cassie had switched the radio on, but there had been no news of any airplanes found for at least three songs worth of air time. Then, once she'd begun applying Alicia's foundation, "Stairway to Heaven" came on, and Cassie relaxed a bit. Surely the deejay would not risk an epic song like that if there was major news to pass on.

While Cassie worked, Alicia shifted into high gear. She began to ask about every detail of Cassie's life, like a forensic examiner eking out information. But it wasn't like in the schoolyard; Alicia was not making small talk. Maybe the kitchen and car revelations had made her curious, but she seemed to be grilling Cassie for evidence. She was also moving her face way too much for makeup application, but how could Cassie tell her to stop talking? This was supposed to be a girls' night out, after all. If only she had some kind of tool to set between Alicia's teeth, like those sharp things they shove into your mouth before a dental x-ray. A bit of pain if she dared to move or speak.

What made you stay here? What gets you up in the morning? When your mother passes, will you leave? The litany rolled on, despite Cassie having covered most of these topics earlier. It seemed like Alicia was trying to have their move to this town make some sort of sense, when clearly, she was miserable.

Cassie answered honestly at first but stopped by the time she got to Alicia's eyeliner. Was it a crime if she made living in Stevens Falls sound better than it actually was? A town is a different world to every person within it—that was something she'd read recently, in a feature on Fort McMurray. Up there, it was more obvious: the newly rich, the drugged-out oil pigs, and young families with all the toys, versus the mourning environmentalists and the indigenous elders who declared the whole landscape dead.

Still, Cassie could not lie. Instead she began to turn it around, asking Alicia what kept her here, other than Iain.

"Nothing," she said. "If he died or got abducted, I'd be gone."

"But what about Chloe?" she asked, shocked to hear this. "She's doing okay here, isn't she, aside from the nature fear?"

Alicia started to say something, then bit it back.

"What?" Cassie asked. She'd just put some colour into Alicia's cheeks. Suddenly she was a happier-looking woman with better bone structure. Someone who would turn heads. Get a job. Relax a little.

"Chloe's never going to be okay, Cassie. She's broken inside."

Cassie dropped the lip liner she was about to use to resurrect Alicia's mouth. She laughed, nervously. "Aww, no, she's a sweet girl."

"No, it's true," Alicia said, evenly. "I think she's beyond fixing."

The word *adopted* floated to the surface of Cassie's brain, but she didn't ask. It was the only explanation that Cassie could think of. Alicia's comment was cruel and dismissive even if what she said were true. Cassie didn't know how any mother, even an adoptive one, could say such a thing. Still, it allowed her scrambling mind to move from incredulous to sympathetic, and it let Alicia—in part, at least—off the hook.

"What . . . what's wrong?"

She thought, Spectrum, maybe, or some kind of mental health issue, drugs in the mother's womb, although Chloe had never shown any indication of that on playdates.

"She's selfish and bossy," Alicia said. "We've given her a perfect life. Right from the fucking water birth to the meditation music piped into her eco-friendly crib, and so on, blah blah blah, and she just doesn't get it."

Cassie's sympathy vanished. Not adopted. Selfish and bossy was not broken. It was the default. Didn't this woman know *anything* about kids?

Suddenly she wanted nothing to do with this makeover. She picked up the lip liner from the floor, but then, made a snap decision: she wouldn't use it. She would leave Alicia's mouth totally naked, a pale hole in the middle of the majesty she'd created.

"All done," Cassie said, just as the radio station sounded its top-of-the-hour chime. The announcer came on and read an update that sounded rushed, almost as if it had been quickly cobbled together by the news team.

Breaking news tonight in what seems to be shaping up as a case of UFO, an as-of-yet unidentified flying object. Earlier this evening it was assumed a plane had crashed near the old quarry. However, no traces of a plane have been located, nor any reports of missing aircraft filed, despite a number of concerned citizens joining the emergency crews in the search. Yet many people swear they saw something bright moving across the sky and falling in the area just off County Road 10. Don Fallis of Fallis Shoes says it was orange, very fast, and streaked across the edge of the sky. And local astronomer Alistair Roberts believes it could have been a meteorite.

At that point the audio cut away to a pre-recorded sound bite recorded over the phone. Roberts spoke for a couple minutes before the clip ended with...

They're called Earth grazers. We can begin a search when day comes. If we're lucky, we'll find it. Magnets will stick to rocks that come to us from space.

The update then switched back to the announcer.

Folks, it may be some time before we know exactly what fell to Earth. In the meantime, here's Jefferson Airplane's 1967 hit, "White Rabbit."

"Weird!" Cassie exclaimed. "A meteorite? But thank God there's no plane down."

Alicia sniffed. "Typical. Small-town panic over what, a shooting star?"

What was that in Cassie's stomach now? Hatred? Indignation? Whatever it was, she wanted it gone.

"How about that drink?" she asked.

"God, yes," Alicia said.

Cassie swept all of the makeup into a shopping bag and hung it on the staff coat rack. Then, she took Alicia out the back door so she wouldn't pelican away more stock in her slouchy purse. Only once they were in the car did she remember that she hadn't shown Alicia her made-up face. Strangely, Alicia hadn't asked to see, but now she turned Cassie's rear-view mirror toward her. "Yowza," she said. "Hot mama."

"You look great," Cassie said, and turned the mirror back toward her before Alicia had time to notice her lips.

|||||||||||||||||||||||||||||||

They went to Wood's, the one place worth going to, its misplaced apostrophe yet another thing Alicia could poke fun at. Heads turned when they went in. There were a couple double takes, and Cassie had to raise her hand and smile at a few patrons. Once they were at a tall table by the window and had pints of pale ale in their hands, Alicia pulled out her phone.

"I still don't give a shit," she said. "It's just habit."

Cassie was glad she was checking. "No messages from the ER?"

"Nope. I'm still surprised that a backwater like this even has a hospital."

What an idiot! Did she expect them all to be as healthy as horses, out here in the fresh country air?

"It serves a large area, actually," Cassie said. "Right up to the edge of Ottawa."

Alicia was gulping down her beer like it was milk. A silence developed between them as they both scanned the room, looking for—what? People looking back?

Not for Cassie. She was looking for escape. Friend, relative, customer, she didn't care—she just wanted another person to generate a nicer conversation.

"Cassie," Alicia said, then tried to disguise a burp with a cough. "I have a confession to make."

Oh, no. Here it comes, Cassie thought. The affair. The alter ego. The drugs she took to mess Chloe up during the pregnancy.

"Okay," she said, forcing herself to sound calm. "What is it?"

"We didn't come here for Iain's toy obsession."

"Oh?"

Alicia leaned closer to Cassie, lowering her voice to a near-whisper. "It was for you. Or people like you." She swept her hand in front of her, taking in the whole bar. "This town. This life. All of it. Iain's writing a big story about it, and we're supposed to pretend he isn't."

Cassie recoiled from Alicia's beery breath. What the hell?

"A story?" She tried to smile it off. "What kind of story? A novel?"

"Well, *story* isn't really the right word. It's more of a . . . an exposé." She shook her head. "I just thought you should know. It was getting too hard to hold it in anymore."

Cassie glanced at Alicia's mouth—her colourless, wrinkle-collecting mouth—smiling like she'd just delivered wonderful news.

"I see," Cassie said. "And what has he found?"

"He won't tell me a thing. Of course, I give him details, but I don't know if he uses them. All I know is that I want to go home. The gig, or the jig, whatever they say, is up. We don't belong here, and I've never been good at acting." She finished her last inch of beer. "Fuck, it feels good to finally tell you. I was starting to feel like I might burst."

Burst? *She* was going to burst? Cassie's body suddenly felt enormous, like a huge balloon being squeezed by the hands of a giant. An aneurysm in waiting. An explosion, pending. And Alicia was watching her, expecting her to say something.

"This is . . . well, it's a lot to take in." It was Cassie's turn to guzzle her pint: the best five-point value of the day, even better than the ice cream.

"It won't paint you in a bad light," Alicia said. "Or if it does, I'll make him change it." She leaned in close again. "But please don't tell Iain I told you. He'll go ballistic."

Cassie nodded. She had to get out of here, especially since she'd just noticed her mother's best friend, Judith, walk in. There was no way she was going to introduce Alicia to the kindest woman in the world. The bitch would likely mock Judith's palsied face as soon as she turned around. "Okay," she said. "Okay. We should probably go soon, hey?"

"So soon?"

"It's getting late for June," Cassie replied. "She'll be a bear tomorrow if we don't get her to bed soon." She didn't care about bedtime: it was the weekend. She just needed to get this woman out of her sight.

Alicia sighed, and started to put on her jacket. "Yeah, Chloe too. But don't you just want to say screw it all? Like, what about our lives? What about what we want?"

"I don't mind," Cassie said, walking toward the back door to avoid Judith. "I like being a mother."

"Well, that makes one of us," she said. "Beam me out of here, and I'd be one happy camper."

||||||||||||||||||||||||||||||||

After they were back in the car, Cassie felt even more wretched. She'd just shared intimate details of her life with this monster, who was going to trot back and report it all to her monster husband. She tried to think rationally about what to do next. She knew she had to do something to get back at Alicia, or get through, but what would possibly match this direct hit to her belief system, her certainty that there was more goodness than evil in the world?

As she was driving out of the pub's parking lot, it came to her. She turned south instead of north, back through a different part of town. She was going to take Alicia on a tour.

There were many ways this could go: a *This is Your Life* kind of thing, à la *Sesame Street*'s Guy Smiley, or a highlights tour of the historically important, or even her own kind of exposé, to make sure Iain got the real story. But was any of that real? There were other types of real. *Realer* real. If these people wanted authentic, they would get it.

Cassie drove toward the edge of town, where a second hospital stood. But this one, slowly sliding into neglect, was about to be shut down for good, despite its residents with nowhere to go and no capacity to choose. The name for the population it served had changed over the years, and now, Cassie believed, it was developmentally delayed, but the people hadn't changed. They were still people, trapped by a curse they could never lift.

Visiting hours were long over, but Cassie was going to drive there anyway, use it as a backdrop for her own story, the one about her two cousins. Thea was still inside, and Joanne was taken there as a child because her parents thought she was damaged goods—just like her sister. Instead, when the doctors could find nothing wrong with her, her parents kept her locked up in the basement most of the time, all because she reacted to too much noise by making her own noises, noises they didn't like. That cousin had just written a book: if Alicia wanted to talk *stories*, well, there was a doozy. The book was about string theory.

They were nearly at the hospital gates when Alicia's phone buzzed. "Oh, great," she said. "Here we go."

And little Chloe was broken? Chloe was the only unbroken one in the family. Cassie's anger was building to dangerous proportions. She started shaking all over.

"Iain just texted. The girls want to have a sleepover. That okay with you, Cass?"

June! Her baby was back at this woman's house, and so was Pete, both unsuspecting players in the play that Iain was watching—and directing. Such effortless acting on their part! Such ease in the role of simple townsfolk, believing in the fun of remote-control cars and potlucks, trapped in a sticky web of pretend hospitality. No, that was not okay with her. And what had she called her, all BFF now? *Girlfriend* before, and now, *Cass*? No. Just no.

She had to rescue her family. The hospital trip would have to wait.

"Sorry," Cassie said, slowing down, then turning the car around to head back to the house, telling her the first lie she could think of. "June doesn't have her medication."

ııııııııııııııııııııııııı

When they got back to the house, Iain looked at Alicia like he'd never seen her before, but he started leering and making kissy sounds. Chloe took one look at her mother and made a face.

"Eww. I don't like it."

"I didn't do it for you," Alicia said.

For whom had she done it? Evidently, not Cassie; it was yet another ploy to get in with the locals. Not for herself—she had scarcely glanced at her face in the car mirror. And not to tempt Iain, although that appeared to be happening right in front of them. But it *must* be Iain she'd done it for. It seemed like Alicia was doing everything for this man—and not enjoying any of it.

After they said their thank yous and goodbyes, they hauled a crying June away from her beloved Chloe and headed back home, and Cassie let Pete tell her all about the ridiculous stuff Iain had in his RC heaven. Her story would need to wait until June was out of earshot.

Even though the drive was less than fifteen minutes, door to door, June fell asleep in the car. After Pete had carried June into her bedroom and tucked her in for the night, clothes still on, Cassie brought a bag of chips and two bottles of beer into the living room and joined him on the couch. He'd already raided the cupboards for mixed nuts and granola bars.

"What kind of meal was that?" he said. "I'm starving."

"You don't even know the half of it."

She drank a couple points worth of beer, and then, she told him everything, from meteorite to makeover to their messed-up intentions. Nearly everything. She left out just how much she had overshared.

As predicted, Pete was pissed off. Once she got to the part about Iain's story, he stood up and started pacing and swearing—a string of impressive names, even for him. Then, it only took him a few minutes to form a clear idea of what to do about it. She'd never seen him grin in quite that way.

"Tell me," Cassie said.

"We'll take them hunting."

"What? Really? Is deer season open already?"

"Not for deer. For fucking meteorites. As if that's really what hit out there."

"You don't believe it?"

Pete laughed. "No. But that doesn't matter. We'll take them on a little tour, give them a little extra bang for their buck."

"What?"

"A local favourite."

Cassie listed the possibilities: the chocolate or cheese factory, the antiques place, cow tipping or cow chip throwing, but it wasn't any of these.

There was that grin again. "You said it hit down by the quarry, right? Well, we're gonna take them there. For a swim."

To anyone else this would sound like code for drowning, but she knew that wasn't Pete's intention. It was simply that—a swim—in freezing cold water, a thing that local people did as a rite of passage, usually when they got drunk enough to have it hurt a little less. Even Pete had gone into the questionable water one night with a local buddy, after he moved to Stevens Falls, just to call himself a part of the community.

After he shared his plan with her, they sat quietly, sipping their beer and picturing the scene they would bring to life the following day.

"It's a good idea," she said. But she had to ask. "Naked?"

"It's November. They won't be packing their swimsuits." Then, he added, gently, "You don't mind, do you?"

Cassie hadn't let him see her fully nude in the daylight for years, but she was getting closer to her goals. Frankly, the chips and beer and ice cream aside, she'd eaten so little all night that it felt like she'd lost a few pounds since lunch. Soon, if things continued to go her way, he would see her waist again, the faint hint of hipbones. Alicia was not a threat, and even if she were supermodel material, Cassie knew Pete was repulsed by her. And was he worried about her seeing Iain? Was any man worried about his wife seeing a naked man in this kind of weather?

"I think I'll manage."

‖‖‖‖‖‖‖‖‖‖‖‖‖‖‖‖‖‖‖‖‖‖‖‖‖

That night, Cassie couldn't fall asleep. She trusted Pete and knew that the plan was in keeping with the Dawsons' local agenda. Still, it played out in her weary head a hundred times, over and over, all variations ending abruptly before the final step.

How had a simple dinner party ended up like this?

Friendliness, that's how. The very thing her mother had always encouraged—those flies with honey, and so on. And what would her mother think, now, of their grand plan?

She would not think it was friendly in the least. But neither was having their lives poked through and made fun of!

It was really just more of a prank than a plan, Pete's idea, better than doing nothing. Wasn't it?

When these thoughts finally settled, the meteorite appeared in her head. Their little town, nearly struck by a giant chunk of rock, hurled from space! The image of it hitting earth made her eyes pop open wide again. If it was true, then they should be celebrating, shouldn't they? Getting off this lucky? No houses destroyed, no one hurt at all?

‖‖‖‖‖‖‖‖‖‖‖‖‖‖‖‖‖‖‖‖‖‖‖‖‖

The next morning, after strong coffee, a few Tylenols, and a couple of phone calls, Pete and Cassie picked up their regular sitter, Brenda, and took her and June out to the subdivision with a three-DVD set of Barbie movies and exchanged them for Alicia and Iain. The pair of them were decked out in sparkling new hiking outfits, but they looked bedraggled when they climbed into the back seat. Cassie could see that Alicia's makeup hadn't been properly removed; she didn't bring it up.

When he called and woke them up that morning, Pete had called it an adventure. He'd told them to bring all their magnets, so they could put them together and help locate the meteorite, and they'd actually done it. They had a bag beside them filled with plastic vegetable magnets and a 3-D moose one—Cassie had seen them the night before on the fridge. She and Pete had brought a few of their own, including a horseshoe magnet, to keep things plausible.

As he drove, Pete started telling stories. Stories, in the old sense—made-up, fantastical tales, flights of imagination—about the area. Tales of his family planting the first lilac trees, of Cassie's family walking with herds of animals and children all the way from Montreal, of his family drifting down the Rideau on rafts. Some were based on truth, at least the seeds of them. Iain kept saying, *that's amazing, that's incredible*, giving Alicia complicit glances all the while.

It started to snow as they turned down Old Quarry Road.

"And so it begins," Iain said. "Father Winter's dandruff."

"God, Iain," Alicia said. "That's a horrid simile."

"Metaphor, darling. Similes use 'like' or 'as.'"

They were both insufferable.

Pete and Cassie were quiet, scanning the side of the road for the trailhead. Once Pete spotted it, he pulled over and killed the engine, then turned to face the back seat. Cassie did the same.

"So," he said, mildly. "Cassie tells me you're writing about this place."

Iain's narrow face turned red. Then, he slapped Alicia's arm with the back of his hand. "How could you?"

Before she could answer, Pete said, "Don't sweat it. We won't say a thing."

"But the whole point was to—" Iain stopped. "It's just—"

"Guys," Pete interrupted, "we want to help you. Show you some local rituals, hidden gems and stuff. Things that won't find their way into the tourist guide."

"You see?" Alicia said. "It's better that they know. They can help you, Iain!"

"I doubt it," Iain muttered. "Dammit, Alicia. We made a deal."

"It's true," Cassie said. "We'll let you in on things no one else will share. Secrets."

What she wanted to share was that she and Pete thought Iain and Alicia were the worst kind of people. Despicable. Having no morals or ethics or scruples in the least. But they'd probably think she was taking all those words from a book under her seat, unlikely, as a local, to be any sort of educated at all.

IIIIIIIIIIIIIIIIIIIIIIIIIIIIIIIII

Through lightly falling snow, Pete led the way down the trail, over dead yellow leaves and a couple of fallen aspens. Alicia followed him, and despite her never having been a Girl Guide, she seemed adept at stepping over the barricades. Iain was not as agile. Cassie brought up the rear, Iain ahead of her, stumbling more than walking and twice nearly causing her to fall before she put another metre between them.

Cassie hadn't been out to the quarry in years, and never this late in the season. November was her least favourite month—the pall of Remembrance Day created an umbrella of sadness over the whole thirty days. But she always felt guilty as soon as she complained about it: sadness was the bloody point.

Pete's plan was simple: to convince them to take an initiation swim, if they really wanted to do what locals did. In exchange, he would tell them much more than they'd ever learn otherwise. After the two idiots had stripped down and jumped into the quarry pool, likely cursing and yelling at the cold, Pete and Cassie would remain on the edge and laugh. Maybe they'd wave their hands in the sign of the cross above the water, for effect, and then, when Iain and Alicia climbed out again, they'd offer them the towels from Pete's backpack, a slap on the back, and a shot of whisky.

Ten minutes of crunching, tripping, and small talk later, in which Cassie tried and failed to keep her worries about the danger of the plan from her head, there they were: a rock pond with walls the colour of orange tabby cats, danger signs posted everywhere, prohibiting trespassers.

"Welcoming sort of place," Alicia remarked.

"Oh, it's not so bad," Pete said. "They just want to keep the kids out."

He left the trail, found the hole in the chain-link fence and waited, holding it open for the rest of them. Alicia and Iain didn't move.

"It's fine," he called. "I want to show you something."

"Really," Cassie said. "There's a story in it."

Once they were all standing a few feet from the edge, Pete made his suggestion, emphasizing the initiation process.

"Prime material," he said. "You'll win awards for this story."

"Not a chance," Iain said, lightly. "That looks like certain death."

"It's all good," Pete encouraged. "You'll be in and out in no time."

Alicia tightened the wool scarf around her neck and turned back toward the trail. "The signs say no. And I thought we were hunting stars, boys. Let's keep going."

"Ah, don't worry about the signs. I've done it lots of times," Pete said. "It'll be over in a couple of minutes. You can climb back up right over there." He pointed at a place in the rock wall that appeared to have a few handholds, a couple of branches hanging over to grab.

Iain snorted. "Sorry, mate. I'm not a mountain goat. Or a fan of pneumonia."

"I brought towels," Pete said. "And whisky."

Cassie should have added her encouragement here, egged them on, but hearing Pete tell them about what he'd brought made her cold to the bone. They could see through them, couldn't they? The plan was flawed. It would never work. And the rocks were orange—nearly brick-coloured! Iain was likely about to have a panic attack, just by being there.

It wouldn't work because Alicia and Iain didn't want to become locals.

They were only there to *use* the locals. To observe, rape, and pillage—and today, more than likely, to make fun of the people who were just half a mile down the road, hunting through the bleak foliage for a nondescript bit of space junk—and get out again, alive. The swimming plan would never work.

Pete must have realized the same thing just then because, at the very moment that Iain stepped around him to take the lead through the woods, Pete's shoulder decided to move toward the quarry. His hip—his well-toned, rink-trained hip—made the same decision. Its thrust sent Iain flailing over the edge and into the frigid, murky water.

Alicia was screaming even before the lip of the splash came up. "Iain! Oh my God, oh my God!"

Below them, they could all hear Iain's gasping, his splashing struggle.

"He'll be okay," Pete said.

"Fuck you!" she yelled. "You pushed him!" She began to pace back and forth along the edge, calling down to Iain for him to swim toward her. "Can you hear me, honey? Up here!"

"He slipped," Pete said. "Didn't you see that?"

But Alicia didn't answer. She'd jumped in after him.

"Oh, shit!" Cassie yelled. "Pete!"

Pete nodded. "They just needed some encouragement."

Below them, Alicia had resurfaced and was swimming toward Iain, who seemed to be treading water, clumsily. "Keep kicking!" she cried. "Don't stop!"

"Over there!" Cassie yelled, pointing to her right, to the easiest way out. "Swim over there!"

But they didn't hear her, or if they did, they didn't care. They began, slowly, to swim toward the other side.

This was bad. Cassie kept her eye on the two swimmers, making sure they were still moving, still had their heads above water. She'd completed her Bronze Cross training eons ago, and remembered enough about rescue—although what could she do from up here? There were a few storm-blown young trees nearby, and she could use one as a pole to reach them if she were on the same level. But she was at least eight feet above them, and there wasn't any shore to get to in a hurry. From what she could see, they were managing to stay afloat.

Her mind was flipping all over the place. Would the police call this kidnapping? It wasn't kidnapping if the people came willingly, was it? And no one would report them missing, either, because they weren't missing. She and Pete weren't trying to hurt anyone. They weren't psychos! This was just tit-for-tat. A prank. A harmless little prank.

Pete called down again, told them to find the natural ladder of rock ledges to help them back up. But they couldn't hear him, either. They were slowly moving away from Cassie and Pete, heading for the far edge of the square hole.

"Maybe there's another way out," Cassie said. "Something they can see from down there."

"No," Pete said. "They're just fucking dumb."

After a minute more of watching the swimmers, Pete wrapped her in a hug from behind. Both of them were very cold, as if they'd been the ones to jump, their toques nearly white with big-flaked snow. They *had* been, metaphorically: the town's name was done for now because of them. It was a terrible plan. But they still had each other, and a child, and a babysitter they would have to rescue from the clutches of that subdivision before Iain and Alicia got there.

Oh, but how would Iain and Alicia even get there, if not with them? This thing had become a complete shit show. They'd made a massive mistake.

Cassie's whole body tightened below her goosebumps. No decision was a good one, no way to sanctify their position, their actions—except one. Cassie pulled away from Pete and took off her coat and shoes.

"I'm going in," she told Pete. Soon Alicia and Iain would be too cold, too tired to continue swimming. She remembered from her training how quickly hypothermia could set in, especially when people panicked. She had to bring them back alive.

"No way," Pete said. "I'll go."

"I float better," Cassie said, and before he could stop her—and before she could talk herself out of it—she pulled her hat down tighter over her head, took a deep breath, and jumped.

She hit the icy water still holding her toque and went down what felt like ten metres before kicking her way madly back to the surface. With her first breath she tried to swear, but the cold turned it to a gasp.

She oriented herself, then waved her hands at Pete and croaked out instructions for him to throw her one of the fallen saplings. He did. She tried to ignore the horribly cold water and the thickening snowfall as she one-arm breast-stroked her way toward Alicia and Iain, the spindly tree beneath the other arm.

"Stop!" she called, every so often, her faint voice growing fainter from the effort, until she was near enough to touch them.

"Stay. Away," Alicia wheezed. "You—two—are—monsters."

Iain was lying on his back, his face nearly blue. Alicia seemed to be pulling him by the sleeve. Both of their heads were barely above the water, and Alicia's pace was slowing by the second.

"You have to come back," Cassie said. "There's no other way out."

"No," Alicia said. "Fuck off!"

"Ladder," Iain croaked.

Cassie looked again at where they were headed. There *was* a ladder, some kind of rope affair against the orange rock. "Oh!" she said. "We couldn't see it through the snow!"

Alicia looked like she could kill her. *Would* kill her, shortly. She had to ignore it, and get this job done.

"Hold on," Cassie said, moving the sapling within Iain's reach.

"He's fine. Iain, don't do it!" Alicia said.

He didn't look fine. He looked, in fact, like he was going to die. Like he would need to be lifted out of the water by ropes tied around his lifeless shoulders. Then there would be a post-mortem in a matter of hours, and the cause of death would be evident in his blood: little fingerprints of evidence that revealed Cassie and Pete, upstanding citizens, to be at the heart of it all. But it wouldn't be true! The beating heart at the centre of this was an accident. A prank gone wrong. A couple, just out to protect the place they loved.

Cassie swam close enough to Iain that she could slide the sapling under the arm that Alicia wasn't pulling. He grabbed on. Suddenly, it seemed, their fury was gone. Alicia let go of Iain, then took hold of the tree as well.

They just wanted to survive. And Cassie, well, she was in charge of everyone. She liked that role, if she was honest with herself; she liked being the one to rescue. That was the crux of her job, wasn't it? Making people's lives better, by rescuing them from dull complexions and rosacea. Bringing out their best, post-chemo, beneath their rented wigs. She was good at her job, task oriented. She got stuff done, and with a smile!

Except that right now, every muscle was turning to stone; every inch of her leaner, lighter body responding less and less to the one task she had to complete. Cassie held her wooden tow-rope as best as she could with her numb fingers and kicked her frozen feet, aiming them all toward the ladder, that miracle hanging there against the rock face, cursing the fat she'd lost, because fat makes you float, and she was less buoyant now, especially with clothes on, and she was sinking, but she felt lighter and yet, somehow, so heavy, her limbs like lead, sinking . . .

Cassie squinted to see the ladder through the gritty snow in her face, and all she could hold onto was one slender thought: if there were meteorite hunters out here, they would be nearby, with warm layers to spare. Because most people born and raised in Stevens Falls had descended from pioneers, or had been Guides or Boy Scouts, at home in nature and always prepared for the worst.

//////// ACKNOWLEDGEMENTS

These stories were written over many years, out of love and com-
pulsion. I am grateful above all for having the affliction/passion/
practice of writing in my life. It has saved me and my relation-
ships on many an occasion.

What else—rather, who else— has saved me? My family, especially my husband, Ryan, and my daughter, Avery Jane. Their
love, their belief in me, and their inspiring focus on creativity
continue to sustain me. My three (!) writing groups—the Fiction
Bitches, the Wildwood Writers, and the Writaminers—have been
by my side, or in my inbox, through it all. Special shout-outs
to Sara Cassidy and John Gould for last-minute editing help
and ongoing friendship, and Traci Skuce, my near-daily writing
partner and friend, who's seen these stories in bits and pieces for
many years and helped me through the muck on many occasions.

The day I signed this book's contract, high fives streaked across
the sky like meteors. I am so grateful to have Brindle & Glass
as my publisher: Taryn Boyd, Tori Elliot, Colin Parks, and the
whole gang at the office; Kate Kennedy, my astute, kind, and generous editor; keen-eyed copyeditors Renée and Warren Layberry;
proofreader Claire Philipson; and talented cover designer Tree

Abraham. Thank you to mentors Annabel Lyon and Elisabeth Harvor for their help on early drafts of a few of these stories, many moons ago, and to my readers: thank you for taking a chance on these stories and their imperfect, oddball characters.

Thanks to the journals *The Rusty Toque*, *The New Quarterly*, *Dreamers* and *carte blanche*, where versions of some of these stories previously appeared. The story "The Expansion" appeared as a stand-alone chapbook after winning the *Rusty Toque*'s 2016 contest judged by Suzette Mayr, and a previous version of "Hangman" placed second in the Rona Murray Competition.

I am grateful for the financial support of the Canada Council and BC Arts Council over the years, for the land on which I write and live in Victoria, BC, which is unceded Coast Salish territory, and for my first home in the Lanark Highlands, ON, unceded Algonquin territory.

JULIE PAUL is the author of two previous short story collections, *The Jealousy Bone* and *The Pull of the Moon,* and the poetry collection *The Rules of the Kingdom. The Pull of the Moon* won the 2015 Victoria Book Prize and was a *Globe and Mail* Top 100 book. She lives in Victoria, BC.